Cursed with a poor sense of direction and a propensity
to read, **Annie Claydon** spent much of her childhood
lost in books. A degree in English Literature followed by
a career in computing didn't lead directly to her perfect
job—writing romance for Mills & Boon—but she has
no regrets in taking the scenic route. She lives in
London: a city where getting lost can be a joy.

HEALING THE VET'S HEART

ANNIE CLAYDON

MILLS & BOON

Published in Great Britain 2020
by Mills & Boon, an imprint of HarperCollins*Publishers*
1 London Bridge Street, London, SE1 9GF

© 2020 Annie Claydon

ISBN: 978-0-263-08797-0

MIX
Paper from
responsible sources
FSC **FSC™ C007454**
www.fsc.org

This book is produced from independently certified FSC™ paper
to ensure responsible forest management.
For more information visit www.harpercollins.co.uk/green.

Printed and bound in Great Britain
by CPI Group (UK) Ltd, Croydon, CR0 4YY

Northamptonshire
Libraries

F

To Stuart
With grateful thanks for simple answers
to complicated questions

CHAPTER ONE

DREW TREVELYAN EASED himself out of his car, pausing for a moment to take a deep breath of sea air. He'd always loved the clarity of early mornings here, the way the sea seemed to stretch out beyond the sheltered curve of the bay in an endless swell of ever-changing colours. When the construction of the new buildings of the Dolphin Cove Veterinary Clinic had been underway, he'd often come here just to sit for half an hour before going on to work in the cramped quarters of the veterinary practice he shared with Ellie Stone…

Drew smiled. A lot had changed in the last few weeks. He'd returned home to Dolphin Cove, after months in hospital and then rehab, to find that his stand-in at the clinic had left. His old friend and Ellie's estranged partner, Lucas Williams, had been Ellie's only option as a replacement and all Drew could do was look on helplessly at the time at the resulting turmoil. Now, another far more joyful turn of events meant that Drew had to remember to refer to Ellie as Ellie Stone-Williams, not Ellie Stone.

The clinic hadn't changed though, and the early mornings here were still as peaceful as they'd been when he and Ellie had first moved in, two years ago. The buildings were starting the long process of becoming one with their surroundings, and moss was beginning to grow on the stone-built technology centre and operating suite on the other side of the ten-acre plot. Here, the wooden frame of the general practice building had begun to mellow, taking on the early autumn colours of the woodlands that lay beyond the drive. The low sun glinted on the high sheets of glass, making them sparkle like the sea.

He was back. Not officially—this visit was a matter of reacquainting himself with a place that he loved, and his diary was as blank as it had been for the last four months. But coming here was one more step that carried him away from the past.

Drew turned, catching up his walking stick and leaning on it heavily as he made his way around to the back of the car, clipping Phoenix's lead onto her collar and lifting the ten-week-old chocolate Labrador down to the ground. She sniffed the air, and then started to tug on the lead, seeming to know that she'd come home too.

Phoenix had been Ellie's idea. A puppy to love and care for, when everyone else around him seemed to think that he should stay down and accept their care. Drew appreciated their concern, but he longed to have a conversation that didn't, at some point, include a solicitous enquiry about his physical and emotional health.

People were kind, there was no doubt about that. They'd been kind when his fiancée had been killed in a diving accident in Puerto Rico two years ago. And when fate had decided that it wasn't done with him yet and the brakes on his car had failed, the village had rallied round again, writing notes and cards and visiting him in hospital. His smashed leg had taken a long time to fully heal, and even now his exercise regime was challenging. But being here gave him a sense of how far he'd come.

'You know where you are, Phoenix?' As he unlocked the main doors to the reception area of the clinic, the puppy started to yelp excitedly, pawing at the glass. 'Not too loud, eh, girl? Ellie and Lucas will hear us.'

There wasn't much chance of Phoenix's barking travelling to the apartment that Ellie and Lucas shared upstairs at the other end of the building. But Drew wanted to be alone here for a moment. He walked into the reception area, past the oak tree that stood in a large tub at its centre. Maybe it was his imagination, but it seemed to have grown a few inches. Nothing else seemed to have changed all that much.

'Everything's fine, Drew. We're managing without you, all you need to do is concentrate on being well again...'

He'd known that was a lie, even if Ellie had told it with the best of intentions. She'd found it hard to keep the practice running without him, and the last few weeks in particular had taken their toll on her. She'd been in turns deliriously happy and deeply despondent, and it had been touch and go as to which would win out.

'Forget it, Drew. Ellie and I will work it out. Stay down for a while...'

Lucas had taken a more direct approach, although the message had been pretty much the same. Lucas and Ellie *had* worked it out, and Drew had been staying down for far too long now. He was more than ready to get back up again.

The deserted reception area smelled of wax polish and hope. The consulting rooms were still the same, one of them filled with a mass of photographs of Ellie's canine patients, and another with a more restrained set of framed photographs that belonged to Lucas. Drew's was…empty. Neat and tidy, without a speck of dust. Drew smiled. It was ready and waiting for him.

'Drew! What the blazes are you doing here?'

Ellie's tone generally became firmer, in proportion to the

size and momentum of the animal she was dealing with. This must be the one she reserved for charging rhinos.

Drew did the only thing possible and let go of Phoenix's lead. When he turned, he saw the puppy barrelling along the corridor, the lead trailing behind her, and Ellie fell to her knees, scooping Phoenix up into her arms. Worked every time.

Or… Every time apart from this one.

'Come on. What *are* you doing here?' Ellie stood to face him, trying not to smile as the puppy licked her neck.

'I could ask you the same question. Shouldn't you and Lucas be staring into each other's eyes over your cornflakes? You are technically still on your honeymoon, even if you are at work.'

Ellie flushed slightly, presumably at the mention of Lucas's eyes. 'You do know what you're doing, don't you? Deflecting one question with another. It so happens that I didn't have cornflakes for breakfast, and Lucas isn't here. He's doing the school run this morning.'

'So you're letting him in gently to the joys of parenthood.' Drew grinned. He imagined that the other parents at the school gate were more of a challenge to Lucas than the whole six years he'd spent as TV's favourite vet.

'He said that yesterday was a bit like running a gauntlet of meerkats.' Ellie shrugged. 'He doesn't mind, really.'

'He loves it. You know that.'

Ellie nodded, smiling. She'd been in love with Lucas ever since the three of them had studied together at veterinary school. Lucas had left to become a celebrity vet, and Ellie had returned to Cornwall, where she and Drew had set up in practice together in Dolphin Cove. When Ellie and Lucas's son, Mav, had been born, he had been so like his father, and a constant reminder that something was missing in all their lives.

But now Lucas was back. Ellie had never loved anyone else, and Drew was happy for them both.

'You *still* haven't answered my question.'

He hadn't counted on springing this on Ellie today, but since she'd asked, he may as well grasp the nettle. 'Why don't we go and sit down in my office.'

'I'm *really* getting worried now. You're trying to butter me up by sitting down, aren't you?'

Drew chuckled. 'Yep. And I don't want Phoenix running around here until she's had her second set of vaccinations.'

He let Ellie tuck his hand into the crook of her elbow, but Drew was careful not to lean on her as they walked. He'd leaned on Ellie far too much already and he appreciated her support, but it had to stop. Leaning on the people around him was beginning to weaken him.

Ellie plumped herself down into a chair, keeping Phoenix on her lap for more cuddles, and Lucas lowered himself into the seat behind his desk. The surface looked as if it had been polished every day while he'd been away.

'I'm coming back to work, Ellie.'

Ellie's eyebrows shot up, but she took a moment to moderate her reaction. 'We weren't expecting you till the end of the month. Are you sure you're well enough? What does your physiotherapist say?'

'She says that if I think I can manage it I should give it a try, just for a couple of days a week for starters. She told me to take things slowly and stop if anything gets too much.'

Relief showed in Ellie's eyes. 'That…doesn't sound so bad.'

'You know I've been going crazy at home, Ells. I really

need this and I'm going to need your support. I know you and Lucas can do with a helping hand here.'

'Yes, we could.' Ellie's gaze softened suddenly. 'Lucas isn't replacing you, Drew. You know that's never going to happen.'

It might. The complex animal surgery Drew excelled at took stamina and strength, and no amount of concentrating on the positive could tell him for sure that he'd ever be able to do that again. But he still had a lot to give, and if anyone *was* going to replace him, he wanted it to be Lucas. And if anyone was going to replace *cool Uncle Drew* in Mav's affections, he wanted that to be Lucas too.

But the late-night fears about being of no more use to anyone were just paranoia. They weren't what Ellie needed to hear from him at the moment.

'You're not the only one who's pleased to see Lucas back, you know. We were all friends, and I've missed him too.'

'You never said…'

Drew rolled his eyes. 'Of course I didn't, not while you were missing him on a completely different level. And being remarkably tight-lipped about it.'

Ellie heaved a sigh. 'Okay. You have my support, just as long as you don't overdo things. If you do, I won't hesitate to escort you off the premises.'

'It's a deal.'

'I suppose…the accounts need signing off.' Ellie shot him a mischievous look. No doubt it had crossed her mind that checking them through involved sitting down.

'I can do that.' Drew called her bluff. 'Although I haven't forgotten that it's your turn this year. Or maybe we should give them to Lucas, since he's our newest partner in the practice.'

Ellie didn't take the bait. 'We'll *both* owe you one, then. Mrs Cartwright's coming in this morning, with Tabatha...'

'Okay. You take Tabatha, and I'll take Mrs Cartwright.' It was well known that whenever Mrs Cartwright made an appointment for someone to look at her cat, she really wanted to sit in the waiting room and chat for an hour. The vets at the Dolphin Cove Clinic always made sure that she got a cup of tea and that someone was available to listen to her.

'You're a darling.' Ellie frowned. 'I suppose you're not allowed to drink welcome-back champagne...?'

'At eight in the morning, and with painkillers, probably not. We'll do that another time.'

'Welcome-back coffee, then? Your mug's in your top drawer....' Ellie gave Phoenix one last hug and got to her feet.

'You go and get on. I'll make the coffee.' Drew opened the drawer of his desk, finding pens and his coffee mug stacked neatly inside. He was going to have to do something about all this tidiness.

'All right.' Ellie planted her hands on his desk, leaning over to kiss his cheek. 'I'm so glad you're back, Drew.'

'Don't get sloppy on me Ells...' Drew could feel a lump forming in his throat.

'Tough guy, eh?' Ellie shot him a speculative look.

'Not really. I just don't want you to get *me* started.'

'That might not be such a bad idea, Drew. You've always been there for me, and now Lucas and I both want to be there for you.'

'You are. And I appreciate it.' He just didn't want to talk about it. 'White no sugar?'

Ellie rolled her eyes. 'That's right. Glad to see you haven't forgotten.'

When Ellie left, he took a moment to soak in the feeling. He was here, sitting behind his desk, and already had a few things to do with his day. Looking at the accounts, making the coffee and chatting to Mrs Cartwright might not be quite at the cutting edge of veterinary practice, but it was a start.

Mrs Cartwright had been delighted to find that one of the vets was prepared to give her his undivided attention for a whole hour. At any moment now Ellie was going to appear and tell him he'd done enough for the day, and Drew had opened the accountant's yearly report in front of him on his desk. If the enticement of having someone else focus their attention on the figures didn't chase her away, then he'd use the bulky folder as a weapon to defend his position.

'Hey. Ellie sent me...' Lucas popped his head around the door, grinning.

'Tell her *no*. I'm perfectly all right here.'

Lucas chuckled. 'You'll have to tell her that yourself, and she's busy charming a snake at the moment.'

Lucas was carrying a bound booklet, which he set down on the desk. Drew peered at the cover page.

'What's this?'

'Remember I told you about the dog prostheses we fitted while you were away? This is the write-up on the operation. The robotics engineer we were working with has some new ideas for an enhanced prosthetic and she'd like to work with us to develop them.' As soon as Lucas sat down, Phoenix bounded towards him, and he bent down to scratch the puppy's ears.

'Thanks. I'd be interested in having a look.' Drew was grateful for his friend's thoughtfulness in asking for his opinion.

'I was rather hoping you'd take charge of it all. I don't have the time.'

'You're sure about this? I can take some of the weight elsewhere, you must want to see it through yourself.' Drew's hand moved towards the booklet and then he pulled it back. The project sounded fascinating, and he was pretty sure that Lucas wanted to steer it himself.

Lucas grinned at him. 'I'd rather not be working during my evenings and weekends at the moment. You'd be doing me a favour.'

'In that case…thanks. I appreciate it.' Drew picked up the booklet and opened it. The introductory page bore the names of everyone who'd worked with Lucas in fitting the prosthetics, including one that he didn't recognise.

'This Caro Barnes… She's the robotics engineer?'

Lucas nodded. 'Yes, I consulted with her on some of my Uber-Vet projects. She's incredibly talented, and one of the few people I wanted to keep in contact with from my time as a TV vet. We struck up a correspondence, and when everything went south on the robotics programme she was involved with in California, she picked up on an off-the-cuff suggestion I'd made, and decided to investigate animal prosthetics. She came back home to the UK, and was in Oxford for a while, fending off various offers for research fellowships.'

'She must be good.' Research fellowships from Oxford University were usually hotly contested.

'Caro's at the top of her field. She can be a little odd at times…'

Drew could handle odd. In fact, the more challenge involved, the better. 'You said she abandoned the robotics programme. What happened there?'

'I'm not sure. Some kind of spat over patents—apparently she lost the rights to something she'd developed. She clearly didn't want to talk about it, and when Caro's not in the mood to talk about something there isn't much point in asking. But she's not one to abandon anything lightly, if that's what you're thinking. She's committed to this project and she'll see it through.'

'You're frowning…' Drew picked up on a note of uncertainty in Lucas's manner.

'When I say she'll see it through, she'll do it in her own way. I find it easier not to ask about her process.'

'Fair enough.' Drew nodded. 'So what does she need from us?'

'I'm not entirely sure. She says she only wants to discuss it on a need-to-know basis, and apparently I don't need to know just yet. I get the impression that this patent business has made her a little paranoid.' Lucas grinned. 'She's living at Smugglers' Top.'

'What?' If anyone wanted isolation then Smugglers' Top was perfect. 'The house up there is in a terrible state, surely she's not living there?'

Lucas chuckled. 'You're behind the times, mate, it's been renovated as a holiday let. Caro managed to get a reduced rate for the whole of the winter.'

'She's serious about her privacy, then.'

'Yeah, Smugglers' Top really suits her. But she's a good sort when you get past the whole mad scientist thing she has going on, and the not speaking to you for days because she's thinking. I went to see her at the weekend and took Mav with me. She gave him a miniature drone with a grab mechanism at the bottom. It's a cool thing, we've been flying it around the apartment, picking things up and putting them down again.'

'I'll bet Ellie *loves* that.'

'There were a few abject apologies after we crashed it into her favourite vase…' Lucas grinned, clearly relishing the apology side of the process. 'You'll have to come over for dinner very soon, Mav can't wait to show it to you.'

Drew wondered if the last bit was a pity gesture, and decided it wasn't. If Lucas had thought that Drew was in need of pity, he would have taken him down to the Hungry Pelican and they could have drowned their sorrows there.

'So… I'm taking on a mad scientist who'll only tell me what I need to know, when she's speaking to me at all, that is, and who lives in an isolated spot that's difficult to get to… Anything else?'

Lucas grinned broadly. 'Nope, that's about it. Are you in?'

Drew chuckled. 'I'm in.'

CHAPTER TWO

DREW PARKED AT the mouth of the gully that led down to the beach. The high outcrop of rock that was known locally as Smugglers' Top was inaccessible at high tide, unless you happened to have a boat. At low tide, it was possible to make the climb up to the house from the beach.

In three hours, the tide would be in, and Smugglers' Top would be completely cut off. But that was enough time to get to the top, meet with Caro Barnes, and get back down again. Drew had spent the whole of yesterday resting at home in preparation for the climb today.

'All right, then, Phoenix.' He opened the back of the car, and the puppy immediately raised her head, sensing that they were about to go for a walk. 'This might be a bit of a stretch for both of us, but we'll make it.'

He slung the canvas bag that contained Phoenix's midmorning snack over his shoulder, and the puppy capered at his feet as he walked slowly across the beach. She had very little appreciation of the adage that slow and steady wins the race, and she'd be exhausted before they got to the top and wanting to hitch a ride.

He was relieved to find that the old steps had new handrails on both sides, fixed firmly into the rock. With the aid of his walking stick, he was able to pull himself up with less effort than he'd anticipated.

All the same, it was a long climb. Ellie had fussed over him, saying that it was impossible he should go all the way up to Smugglers' Top, but he'd cordially ignored her suggestion that he take up Caro's offer of meeting at the veterinary centre in favour of meeting Caro on her own turf. There was no better way of getting the measure of someone.

'We're going to take a rest now…' They were halfway up, and the pup was beginning to tire. Lucas sat down on the stone steps, taking Phoenix onto his lap. After a couple of minutes the pain in his leg began to subside, and the top didn't seem quite so far away.

'Next time it'll be less trouble, eh?' Drew had fallen into the habit of thinking that his own recuperation ran approximately parallel to Phoenix's development. One day soon they'd both be able to walk for a day without having to take a rest.

But right now Phoenix couldn't climb any more. The puppy was curled up in his arms, shielded from the wind, and looked to be snoozing. Protecting her made him feel strong again. Drew opened the canvas bag, pulling out the baby carrier he'd brought with him and fixing the straps under his coat. It was perfect for carrying a tired puppy when you needed both hands to support yourself, and he felt Phoenix snuggle gratefully against his chest.

Another rest seemed in order at the top of the steps, because pride dictated that Caro's first impression of him shouldn't be to find him collapsed on her doorstep. He took the opportunity to extricate Phoenix from the baby wrap, and she began to caper around at his feet. Smugglers' Top was much as he remembered it from playing here as a child. Trees were gnarled and bent in the wind, and hid a dilapidated stone house. But there was a newly laid path from the top of the steps and as he approached the house, he could see that was different too. The old boards that covered the doors and windows were gone now, in favour of a brightly painted door and triple glazing. The thick walls had been cleaned and there was a new slate roof. The place looked positively homely.

Oddly enough, there was a doorbell. Casual callers were unlikely in this isolated spot, and leaving the front door unlocked for an expected visitor seemed the more practical option. But when he lifted the latch and pushed the door with his finger it didn't move, so he rang the bell.

He was starting to wonder whether the bell was actually working and thinking about trying it again when the door flew open. The words *mad scientist* flew at him like a missile.

Caro Barnes was a head shorter than him. Blonde hair, some of which was caught up in a messy plait, with the rest pushed behind her ears. She was wearing a pair of sweatpants that had probably been red once but were now a washed-out dark pink, along with a T-shirt and a large green cardigan that dwarfed her small frame.

'Ah! Sorry! You're…um…' She pressed her lips together, looking up at him.

'Drew Trevelyan. Maybe I'm a little early…?' Drew looked at his watch. He was actually five minutes later than the time they'd arranged.

'Um… No. Probably not. I was working on something and I forgot the time…' She shrugged helplessly, as if that was something that happened a lot. 'Come in.'

She stood back from the doorway, watching uncertainly as Phoenix nosed her way inside. When she went to sniff Caro's fleecy slippers, Caro stepped back suddenly.

'This is nice. A bit different from the way I remember it.' Drew decided that introducing her to Phoenix could wait as Caro obviously wasn't used to being around dogs.

'You know this place?' Caro frowned suddenly. 'I suppose you must do, since you live around here.'

'Yes, I used to play up here when I was a boy. This house was deserted and very ramshackle then.'

'You've always lived here, then?' Caro was looking at him as if he came from another planet. Which wasn't an entirely unpleasant sensation, as her eyes were wide and brown, the colour of dark honey. Knowing and beautiful, all at the same time.

That was entirely irrelevant. Imagining how her hair might shine if she gave it a brush was also irrelevant. He was here to appreciate Caro's intellect.

'Yes, I'm a Cornishman, born and bred.' That was a matter of some pride to Drew. 'I grew up in Dolphin Cove.'

'That sounds nice, growing up somewhere.' Caro frowned, as if the sentence didn't entirely cover all of her intended implications. 'I mean… I grew up, of course. In quite a lot of places.'

'That sounds nice too.' The sudden urge to make her feel at ease gripped Drew. 'Lucas tells me you were working in California before you came here?'

'Yes.' Caro didn't seem to want to elaborate on that. 'I'll get you some coffee and…um…freshen up if you don't mind. I'll only be five minutes.'

It occurred to Drew that Caro had probably been up all night, working on something, and he suppressed the urge to tell her that whatever it was could probably have been done just as well after a good night's sleep. How she chose to organise her life was none of his concern.

'Take your time. I can make the coffee if you show me the way to the kitchen.'

'No. That's all right.' Caro's glance flipped to his walking stick. 'You should probably sit down. I actually really wish you would, it'll make me feel a bit better for bringing you all the way up here and then answering the door in my pyjamas.'

Somehow, the invitation to sit didn't carry with it the tang of frustration and humiliation that it usually did. Standing next to Caro made him feel strong and steady, in a way he hadn't felt for a long time now. And she was charming, in an odd kind of way. Nakedly honest, although he really shouldn't include the word *naked* in any sentence that referred to her. The green cardigan seemed to be inviting him to imagine the figure it so effectively hid.

She waved him towards a pair of sofas that stood next to the hearth, at one side of the open-plan living area. Drew sank down onto the cushions, trying not to heave a sigh of relief and keeping Phoenix on her lead so that she didn't wander off and get under Caro's feet. The pup sprawled out on the hearth rug, her gaze following Caro as she skittered nervously into the kitchen area.

The conversion had been nicely done. The ceiling beams were new, but the oak would mellow with time. The large space was divided into two by a breakfast bar, and the pale colours in the kitchen and on the walls of the sitting area made everything seem spacious and clean. Wooden floors and the pale, natural tones of the furnishing fabrics added a touch of warmth.

And the house looked entirely unlived-in. Nothing was out of place, not even the cushions on the sofa. It was as if Caro had been parachuted in here to add a little delicious mess to her magazine-cover surroundings.

She was banging the doors of the kitchen cupboards, obviously looking for something while the coffee brewed. Drew watched as she stood on her toes, reaching to the back of one of the units and bringing out a packet of chocolate biscuits.

'Would…um…he like some biscuits?' She pointed towards Phoenix, who returned her gaze steadily.

'She. Her name's Phoenix. She shouldn't have chocolate.'

Caro frowned, tipping half a dozen biscuits onto a plate and then adding a few more for good measure. 'What does she eat, then?'

'She loves cheese, if you have any.' Phoenix's ears began to twitch at the mention of the word, and Drew wondered whether he should have spelled it out.

'Oh! Really? I've got cheese…' Caro fetched two large blocks of cheese from the fridge, and Phoenix jumped to her feet. 'Which does she prefer? Extra mature, or mild and creamy?'

Phoenix wasn't a connoisseur, she just liked cheese. 'Mild and creamy will be fine.' Caro unwrapped the package, hovering her knife somewhere in the middle of the block. 'Not that much. Just a few small squares.'

Caro shrugged, cutting some squares of cheese and putting them onto a saucer. 'What made you call her Phoenix?'

Drew resisted the temptation to say that not everything had a meaning attached to it. In Caro's world, he suspected it did. 'I guess…she's helping me rise from the ashes.'

'Nice thought. Rising from the ashes is always good.'

Drew wasn't entirely sure what she meant by that, but Caro didn't seem to think that the comment required any further explanation. She poured two cups of coffee, taking a quick swig from hers before balancing the biscuits and cheese on top of the mugs to carry them over. As she set everything down on the coffee table, Phoenix decided to stake her claim and came to nuzzle at her hand.

Caro pulled her arm back quickly. If she was going to be studying animals, and her work in making prosthetics made that inevitable, she was going to have to get over her nervousness.

'She won't hurt you.' Drew smiled, picking up one of the squares of cheese. 'Why don't you give it to her?'

Caro shot him a querying look, and he flattened his hand, perching the cheese on top of his fingers to demonstrate. She nodded, sitting down cross-legged on the hearth rug and holding her hand out. Phoenix was keeping her eye fixed on the cube of cheese and her head arced round as he placed it on Caro's fingers.

'Oh!' Phoenix wolfed down the treat, and started to lick Caro's hand, on the off chance she'd left anything behind. 'I thought her tongue would be raspy, like a cat's...'

Drew couldn't remember the first time a dog had licked his hand. And he couldn't imagine a childhood that wasn't surrounded by all kinds of animals.

'You haven't been around dogs much?'

Caro pressed her lips together, as if slightly embarrassed by the question. 'No, not much.'

'But you're spending a fair bit of time and energy making animal prosthetics.'

'Yes. I always wanted a dog when I was little, but I couldn't have one because my parents moved around so much.' She gave a little smile. 'So I made my own. I built my first robot dog when I was ten. It couldn't do much, and one of its legs kept falling off, but I really loved it.'

'But you couldn't feed it treats.' Drew put another square of cheese onto her hand. Almost as soon as he'd done so, Phoenix ate it, and then climbed onto Caro's lap.

'No. I could probably make one now that responds to treats. She smells them, I suppose...' Caro's mind was obviously exploring the possibilities, and she started to examine Phoenix carefully, parting her coat with her fingers. 'She's so soft...'

'She still has her puppy coat. In a couple of months she'll start to shed that, and she'll grow a double layer coat. The top layer is waterproof with a warm underlayer.'

'Hmm. I'd like to see that.' Phoenix had mistaken scientific enquiry for love and was nuzzling at Caro's chin. Perhaps Drew was the one who was mistaken, and love and science weren't so different for Caro.

'You probably wouldn't like vacuuming up all the dog hairs. They get everywhere.'

'Oh, that's all right, I have a tortoise… Tony does my vacuuming for me.'

Drew decided not to ask. Caro's attention was all on Phoenix, and she was stroking her carefully. There was the kind of magic about it that brought a lump to his throat.

'I've…um, I've got to move.' Caro looked up at him questioningly.

'That's all right. Just push her off your lap, she'll get the idea.'

Caro gently pressed her fingers against Phoenix, and the pup ignored her completely. Drew grinned. 'You need to be a bit firmer with her… Phoenix, come here.'

Phoenix took no notice of him, clearly reckoning that Caro was far more interesting. He held out another square of cheese, and Phoenix scrambled off Caro's lap to reach him.

Caro got to her feet. 'I won't be long…' She swiped two of the biscuits from the plate, putting them into the pocket of her green cardigan. Then she picked up another, taking a bite from it as she walked towards a door that led from the open-plan living area to the other side of the house.

Phoenix was eyeing him with that *I-haven't-eaten-in-months* look, and he put the saucer containing the last cube of cheese on the floor. She wolfed it down and started to lick the saucer. Drew took a gulp of coffee, almost choking it was so strong. If this, and her obvious requirement for calories, was anything to go by, Caro definitely *had* been up all night.

Not his business. Not even close to being within his remit as a professional consultant. And however entrancing Caro contrived to be, or rather didn't contrive to be because it was quite obvious that she had no idea just how fascinating she was, *professional* was the word that should cover every aspect of their relationship. He'd made his mind up about that.

He had good reason. Drew had loved Luna with all his heart. He'd only hesitated in proposing to her because his own parents' marriage would give anyone pause for thought. But when Luna's shining optimism, her enthusiasm for the here and now had led her to propose to him, Drew hadn't hesitated to accept.

He'd grieved for her when she'd died. Had gone through all of the stages, starting with disbelief then pain and guilt. He'd blamed himself for not being able to persuade Luna to work a little less and blamed her for diving when she'd been tired from travelling and should have waited a day.

Finally, he'd come to accept it. Luna had been very different from him, she'd travelled the world with a team of conservationists, seeking out catastrophes, while Drew had concentrated his efforts on long-term projects here in Cornwall. They'd both worked hard, but Luna would push herself beyond her limits, never satisfied with what she'd already achieved.

Love wasn't enough. Living together for more than six weeks at a time was the real test, and Luna and Drew had never done that. Their relationship had been a succession of promises to miss each other every night that Luna was away, followed by joyful reunions.

He stretched his limbs, rubbing his face. It was all in

the past now, and Drew's relationship with Luna had been more like his parents' than he'd thought. They had been different too and had argued their way through twenty-three years of marriage, until they'd finally come to the conclusion that they liked each other far better now that they were divorced.

Caro was obviously just as blinded by her work as Luna had been. She was enchanting, beautiful and they were like chalk and cheese. He should remember that the next time he felt the impulse to reach out and touch her.

When Caro reappeared, he hung onto that thought as tightly as he'd gripped his walking stick on the way up here. Her cheeks were pink from the shower, and her hair *was* shining, all of it caught back in a newly-braided plait. She wore jeans and a fresh T-shirt under the same green cardigan and was holding two sheets of paper as if they were about to burn her.

'I've…um…got something for you to sign. There are two copies, one for you and one for me. It's just a… I showed it to Lucas and he was happy with it.' She put the paper down on the coffee table and fished a pen from her pocket.

If Lucas was happy with it, that was enough for Drew. He reached for the pen and Caro started, a look of panic on her face. 'You should read it first!'

Fair enough. Drew focussed on the words on the page, reading them through carefully.

'So, according to this, the work we do here is confidential.' That was as he'd expected, but the final clause was surprising. 'And any designs you produce will be available to others under a creative commons licence. I was assuming you'd hold the rights to your own designs.'

'I want them to be of use to as many people as possible.

This agreement means that you can't assume any rights that would prevent me from doing that.'

The idea hadn't occurred to Drew, and he suspected it hadn't occurred to Lucas either. But Caro seemed unwilling to trust in that, and her plan to allow anyone to use her work free of charge was more than generous.

'You're sure you want to do that? Holding the patent would mean you'd make some money from your work.'

'I have an income from other patented work I've done. I don't need any more, and this is…a holiday.'

'A holiday?' Drew raised his eyebrows and Caro shrugged.

'It's what I love the most. And there's a beach down there, isn't there?'

Right. Drew would lay odds that Caro hadn't explored the beach or her tiny island home. He reminded himself that it wasn't his business what she chose to do on this so-called holiday, and that if she just wanted to work then that was entirely up to her. He couldn't deny the potential benefits to the veterinary community.

'Okay.' He picked up the pen. 'Can I sign now?'

'Yes. Please do.' She allowed herself a smile. 'Now that you know exactly what your responsibilities are.'

As far as Drew could see, his responsibilities extended to not meddling with Caro's generosity. He had no problem with that. He picked up the pen, signing both pieces of paper, and Caro snatched one up.

'Right, then. I'll show you where I am with everything… Ew!'

Drew followed Caro's gaze and saw that Phoenix had taken advantage of the fact that he wasn't looking and was pretending that the puddle she'd made was nothing to do with her. Luckily she'd chosen the tiles in front of the hearth…

'Oh. I'm sorry, I should have taken her outside. I'll clean up—do you have an old cloth and some disinfectant?' Drew got to his feet as quickly as he could manage.

'That's okay. Tony'll deal with it. Tony!'

Before Drew could ask, the sound of whirring caught his attention. Out of the corner of his eye he saw something shoot across the floor towards him, and he stepped aside to get out of its way. The small, tortoise-shaped machine stopped at Caro's feet, and a little head poked out from under the textured carapace.

'Tony. Liquid spill. Hearth.'

The little creature—because it was hard to see it just as a vacuum cleaner—responded immediately. Zipping over to the hearth, it seemed to be searching for the puddle, and when it sensed it another whirring sound indicated that it was dealing with it.

'That's…impressive.'

'He's just a prototype.' Caro was smiling fondly. 'I think I might make him move a little slower. As he's a tortoise.'

'And it responds to your commands.'

Caro nodded. 'And to my voice. Try calling him.'

It felt a little odd, but Drew called the vacuum cleaner's name. It ignored him completely, its mechanical mind set on sucking up the spill and then buffing the tiles of the hearth.

Phoenix was keeping her distance, crouched on the floor, clearly wondering what this was. But she overcame her mistrust quickly and padded up to Tony, her nose twitching. When she extended her paw, the whirring stopped, and the tortoise head moved back and forth, seeming to try to sense the source of the movement. Phoenix took that as an invitation to be friends and pawed at Tony's shell.

'Tony. Go to the kitchen.' Caro issued another command, and the tortoise pushed slowly past Phoenix. As soon as the puppy was out of range it gathered speed, shooting back towards the kitchen. Phoenix was caught up in the game, racing after it and trying to make friends again. Tony slowed down when Phoenix approached, moving gently from one side to the other as the puppy jumped around.

Drew chuckled. 'Outstanding. Does the vacuuming *and* plays with the dog.'

'Tony doesn't know what a dog is. He's got sensors that make him respond whenever something moves close by, it's a safety thing. Phoenix is just confusing him.' Caro called out another command. 'Tony. Sleep.'

The tortoise stilled, but Phoenix still wouldn't let it alone. Drew called her, and she ignored him completely. She could take a few lessons in obedience from her new mechanical friend.

Caro seemed suddenly unaware of his existence too, watching Tony and Phoenix thoughtfully. It occurred to Drew that perhaps she was considering extending Tony's range to take in play, but at the moment Phoenix looked as if she was trying to tip the vacuum cleaner over. He walked across to the kitchen, shooing Phoenix away.

'Interesting…' Caro seemed to be making the observation to herself, and then her gaze found Drew. 'I'll think about that later. Come and see what I'm doing.'

She led him towards what seemed to be the back door of the house, but when she opened it, it revealed a bright, warm conservatory overlooking the sea and protected from the wind by triple glazing.

The magazine-cover neatness of the rest of the house suddenly made sense. *This* was Caro's home—the rest was just a collection of things that might come in useful from time to time. The large space had been cleared of furniture and boasted a row of benches, some at sitting height and others standing. The standing ones were piled up with various electrical and mechanical components, in various states of assembly. There were two large computer screens, piles of books and papers, and the small lobby that led out to a path that ran behind the house contained a large 3D printer. The overall impression was of a mad scientist's lair.

At the far end was a sofa, with cushions piled at one end and a throw tumbled at the other. If Caro *had* had any sleep last night, it had probably been right here.

'Sit.' She marched over to the sofa, quickly clearing the throw and spreading the cushions. Drew sat down, and Caro pulled up one of the office chairs. He caught a faint thrill of her scent as she leaned across to put a thick, spiral-bound booklet on the sofa beside him. *Initial Design Specification for Animal Prosthetics.*

'You can take it home to read. As long as you don't show it to anyone…'

'Of course not. I signed an agreement, remember?'

She nodded, obviously pleased that *he* remembered. Caro jumped to her feet, gathering up a selection of components from one of the workbenches and setting them out on the small table in front of him. Then she reached for a laptop, opening it and tapping on the keys.

'Before you start reading, I'd like to show you these…'

At first, it seemed like a jumble of concepts. Models of human and animal limbs, wire-frame computer rendering, and explanations that seemed to defy limitations that Drew had taken for granted. Then, slowly, he began to get it…

'You're saying that you want to make a prosthetic that can respond to the movements of an animal.' Drew hadn't seen anything like this even attempted before. 'It sounds almost impossible.'

'The possible is only something that's already been done.'

There was a light in her honey-brown eyes that made Drew shiver. Walking past the realms of the possible and making the impossible work seemed suddenly as if it was the only thing he wanted to do. And he wanted to do it very much with Caro.

CHAPTER THREE

WHAT WAS IT with vets? Ellie was gorgeous, in a way that Caro had never even hoped to be. Lucas was handsome, good at his job, and it didn't take him as long as most to get his head around extreme possibilities. She'd imagined that Drew would probably be a counterbalance to their dazzling attractiveness, since every extreme implied that another extreme should restore the sum of its parts to the average.

But Drew didn't do anything to confirm that theory. He wasn't merely handsome, or gorgeous, he was amazing. His voice was softened by a Cornish burr, and those blue eyes seemed to take in everything. Dark curls gave him a slightly windblown look even when he was inside, and he had a body to die for, even if it was a little stiff and battered at the moment. Even that was thrillingly attractive, and Caro wondered how he'd feel about playing the patient while she played the nurse.

That would lead to consequences. Inevitable ones that Caro wasn't prepared to face. Leaving America, and what had become the only home she'd ever really had, and coming back here had been her way of saying an irrevocable goodbye to matters of the heart. Her work was the only thing that mattered.

He was turning the prosthetic that Lucas had used at the clinic over in his hands, examining it carefully. He seemed to get it. The work that had gone into it, and where it could be improved. His obvious approval sent a throb of desire through her whole body.

'So…where do we start?' He looked up at her.

With the eyes. She could start by staring into his eyes. Or with his hands. So gentle in such a strong man…

'Work's already been done on how dogs and other animals move. I want to take those findings and add to them to give me an idea of how the natural movement of a dog might control a prosthetic.'

He nodded, frowning. Obviously applying his mind to the problem. Caro wondered if his mind was as beautiful as the rest of him.

'So the joint will have the ability to flex, in response to the animal's movements, rather than being rigid like this one.'

He got it. A warm swell of gratification filled Caro's chest, before she'd had a chance to remind herself that someone who appeared to *get it* had still been capable of betraying her.

'Yes, that's right.' Her voice sounded a little squeaky and she cleared her throat.

'And the first thing you need to do is capture the movements of real dogs and quantify that, using the software you showed me.' He nodded towards her laptop, and the camera that lay beside it on the table.

He *definitely* got it. Maybe Caro was hallucinating, and she'd find something wrong with this guy when she'd had a good night's sleep and something more to eat than just three chocolate biscuits.

'Yes. I'm hoping to film real dogs and then use the software to quantify their movements.'

Drew nodded. 'How do your robot dogs move? Can you show me?'

Oh, yes. She could show him.

'Clarice!' She called her robot, who she preferred to think of as a *proper* puppy, despite the presence of the wriggling reality at Drew's feet. Clarice was in sleep mode in the corner of the room and raised her head in response. 'Come here.'

Clarice trotted across the room. A lot of work had gone into that gait, but it wasn't quite the same as Phoenix's unpredictable movements. Caro stroked Clarice's head, and when she nuzzled against her legs Caro saw Drew's eyebrows shoot up.

'It responds to you?'

'*She* responds...'

'Sorry. Do that again, will you?'

Caro stroked Clarice's head again and this time she pawed at her legs. 'Her programming mimics real life. She learns, and she has a range of different reactions to any one action.'

'She learns?' Drew shook his head. 'How does she do that?'

'The same way we do. If she responds the way I want her to I reinforce it with my approval.' Caro bent down, stroking Clarice's head again. 'Clarice, well done.'

Maybe she'd gone too far. Moving around so much as a child had meant that Caro's only permanent companions had been her robots. She knew they weren't human, or even proper animals, but sometimes they felt a great deal more dependable. She expected that Drew would think the way most people did and consider that giving her love to a mess of circuitry and plastic was a character flaw. His derision would be harder to bear than usual and betraying her feelings for Clarice would be a mistake.

'It's fascinating. Challenging...' He held his hand out

to Clarice and her head swivelled towards him. 'She's very cute.'

'She's *programmed* to be that way. I could equally easily programme her to snap and growl at you.'

He laughed. 'Then you programmed her well. Maybe that scrap of humanity I see in her is really yours.'

Was he for real? How did he understand that Caro felt that she'd put a little of her own personality into Clarice? She felt herself blush.

Perhaps working with someone who knew nothing about robotics wasn't going to be like wading through mud after all. Drew seemed to understand the bare bones of what she was trying to do.

'So our first challenge is to find dogs to film. I imagine that'll be where *I* come in.'

Caro had been thinking that it was more a matter of what challenges *she* would face. In the singular. The vets at the veterinary centre were just there to provide her with the things she needed. But she couldn't resist those eyes. Suddenly it didn't seem so bad to share some of the challenges with Drew.

A loud beep sounded, and he pulled his phone from his pocket.

'That's my alarm call. The tide's coming in.'

Oh. Up till now, the tide coming in had seemed like a good thing. Something that naturally cut a visit short and allowed Caro to get on with her work in peace.

'That's a shame. We were just getting to the interesting part...' She turned the corners of her mouth down. The interesting part was actually Drew at the moment, and he had to go.

He looked at his phone speculatively, not meeting her gaze. 'It'll be going back out again this afternoon.'

That sounded like an opportunity that was there for

the grabbing. 'Would you like to stay? I'm…um…getting a bit hungry…'

He grinned. 'When did you last eat? Something other than chocolate biscuits.'

Caro thought back. 'Yesterday.' Sometime yesterday, at least. Perhaps he'd jump to the conclusion that she'd had a hearty home-cooked meal yesterday evening.

'Okay.' Drew didn't seem to be jumping to any conclusions. 'I can go out and get us something before the tide comes in, and let you get on with what you're doing.'

'I have plenty of food in the fridge…' Lack of supplies wasn't the issue. Tearing herself away from her workshop to go and prepare a meal was sometimes tricky. 'Would you like some cheese on toast?'

'Sounds good, thank you. Why don't you let me do that? I could do with stretching my legs.'

He never mentioned being in pain, or finding it difficult to walk, but Caro had caught him wincing a few times when he'd thought she wasn't looking. If her little secret was the last time she'd eaten a proper meal, then his might be that he'd be pulling painkillers out of his pocket as soon as he was alone.

'If you don't mind. That would be really nice, thank you.'

'My pleasure.' Phoenix raised her head as he got to his feet, and he bent stiffly to stroke her head. 'Maybe you can persuade Phoenix to let you film her…'

Maybe. Caro picked up the camera, but as Drew walked out of the room, it wasn't Phoenix that she started to film. It was him.

Cheese on toast apparently took a little longer than two minutes to half-melt the cheese under the grill, and when Drew called her out of her workshop, the cutlery laid out on the breakfast bar was an unequivocal hint that she

wouldn't be eating at her desk. But it was actually worth
it. The bread was crispy and there was ham underneath
a golden layer of toasted cheese. And there was coffee as
well, even if the way Drew made it didn't take much of
the edge off her tiredness.

'She's not having cheese for lunch?' Phoenix had scam-
pered through from the workshop with her at the sound of
Drew's voice, and was currently demolishing the contents
of a feeding bowl on the floor.

'No, cheese is a treat. She has a properly balanced formula, four times a day.'

'Right.' Caro eyed the fruit bowl that Drew had placed
next to them. Apparently, he was aiming for a properly balanced formula for her as well. She'd be willing to bet that
if given the chance he'd be an *eat-your-vegetables* freak.

Although the results of vegetable freakery bore thinking
about. With the obvious exclusion of his leg, he looked out-
rageously outdoorsy, well rested and healthy. His strength
might well be the kind to impress a girl indoors too.

'Have some more.' Drew was still on his first slice of
ham and cheese, presumably chewing each mouthful the
prescribed number of times. Caro hadn't been able to stop
herself from wolfing her two slices down and wishing
that there was more. Drew tipped his second slice onto
her plate.

'No…um…that's okay. Aren't you hungry?'

'I had breakfast.' Somehow he managed to avoid making that sound like an accusation.

'In that case…' She picked up the slice. 'This is really
good. I'm a bit tired, and I get hungry when I'm tired.'

He nodded. 'Yeah. Your body's looking for a quick up-
tick in energy. High-calorie foods will fool it into thinking
it has that for a while.'

Okay. He was beginning to sound like her mother. Caro

could ignore that for the time being, since he didn't look anything like anyone's mother. She wondered whether pheromones were fooling her body into thinking she wasn't tired as well.

'I get an idea and I run with it. That's the way it works.'

He nodded, picking up an orange from the fruit bowl. 'Want some?'

Peel me an orange. Not quite so obviously seductive as *Peel me a grape*, but it still allowed her to appreciate the delicate precision of his strong hands.

'Yes. Thanks.'

He deftly stripped the peel from the orange segments, putting more than half on her plate. Was there *anything* that Drew Trevelyan did that didn't bear a closer look?

'You broke your femur. Along with your patella?' She could see through all the things he didn't say, just as clearly as he seemed to see through her.

Drew stared at her, suddenly tense. 'What?'

'I caught you on film. I was going to try filming Phoenix's movements while you made lunch.' Suddenly this felt like an intrusion rather than a reply to his fixation with her diet and how much she slept. Maybe she should have asked first.

'And you got that just from my gait? That software's pretty good, then.'

'It doesn't catch everything. But, yeah, it's pretty good at picking up deviations from the norm.' She shouldn't have done this. 'Sorry. Sometimes I forget that everything isn't an exercise in logistics.'

'Yeah. This is a lot more personal.' He shot her a warning look.

'Like wanting to know when I last slept?'

For a moment she thought he was going to take offence. Then suddenly he laughed. It was a nice laugh that emphasised a *with* instead of an *at*, and Caro couldn't help smiling.

'Touché. It's just like that. And I *am* impressed with the logistics, I think they could be very useful.' He reached for the jug of coffee and refreshed both of their mugs. 'I was in a car accident.'

'Lucas told me. He didn't say that you had trouble walking, I would have come down to the veterinary centre for this meeting.'

Drew shook his head. 'Then I would have missed the delights of your workshop.'

It sounded like a compliment, and Caro decided to take it as one. 'Thanks. I like it too. A bit too much sometimes...'

He nodded, as if he'd already come to that conclusion himself. Caro wanted very badly to know what had happened to him but didn't dare ask.

'The brakes on my car failed. I was on a coast road, and I managed to avoid plunging off a cliff and ended up in a headlong collision with a tree.'

Caro took a gulp of her coffee. She was too tired to filter her reactions through the fine mesh of what was appropriate, but maybe that wasn't such a bad thing. 'It sounds horrible.'

'Yes, it was.' His hand shook a little, and he glared at it as if it had betrayed him. 'I broke my femur, and my patella's been partially replaced.'

'It must hurt you still.'

'Yes, it does. You're very direct.' Drew smiled suddenly, as if that wasn't a problem.

'Sorry. I don't mean to pry.'

He shrugged. 'That's okay. I sometimes wish that everyone would be a bit less tactful.'

So she didn't have any tact? If that was true, she'd have

already made many more personal enquiries about his body, somewhere along the lines of whether it was actually as beautiful as it seemed.

'If we're going to be having business meetings, then it would be easier if you told me what you can and can't manage. Then I wouldn't have to guess.'

He seemed to like that approach. Drew reached across to the canvas bag he'd brought with him and took a blister pack from one of the small pockets at the front.

'I have prescription painkillers, but I'm scaling them down. I only take them when I need them.'

'Like now?' The blister pack had two tablets missing.

'Yeah. I'm still struggling a little with climbing steps.'

'You might have said. We could have made other arrangements…' Caro wrapped her thick cardigan around her, as if the warmth might be of some comfort to the guilty feeling of letting Drew come all the way up here.

'I'm a little tired of being the one that everyone else has to make their arrangements around.' There was a trace of annoyance in his voice.

'Okay, so if I promise not to mention sitting down or taking things easy, will you promise to mention if things really are getting too much for you?'

Drew smiled suddenly. 'That sounds like an excellent work arrangement.'

Did he think that was all it was? Caro suspected that Drew was made for play as well as work, but she'd already experimented with mixing work and pleasure, and the results had been conclusive. Big, bad mistake.

But she was really too tired to think about it. Her back and legs were aching from fatigue and she wanted to sit down on the sofa. Walking across the room seemed like a gargantuan effort, but it would be worth it just to sink into the cushions for a few minutes…

* * *

Someone was calling her name. Caro was wide awake before she even realised she'd been asleep, sitting up before
she'd known that she was lying down on the sofa. Maybe
he hadn't noticed that she'd dropped off. Caro hoped she
hadn't given the game away by snoring.

Only… The throw from her workshop was spread over
her legs. Her slippers were lined up neatly on the floor.
And she was sure that she felt a pillow crease on her cheek.
She decided to brazen it out.

'So…what do you think?' That was always a good holding question. People were always happy to expound for
ages on what they thought and it was a good opportunity
to catch up if her mind had wandered.

Drew grinned. 'I think your ideas are great. I've just
been reading about them.' He indicated her design specification, which lay open on the coffee table. He either read
at the speed of lightning, or her eyes had been closed for
more than five minutes.

Caro puffed out a breath, bowing to the inevitable.
'I've been asleep, haven't I?' She craned around so that
she could see the kitchen clock, focussing blearily on it.
Three o'clock?

He nodded, getting to his feet. Clearly he'd been resting too, because his movements were more fluid than they
had been.

'I'm so sorry…'

Drew shrugged, as if it was just one of those things.
'You were very tired. I would have let you sleep longer,
but the tide's on its way out again, and I should be making a move soon.'

'Okay. Give me two minutes, and I'll walk down with
you.' Maybe she could carry his bag or something. Any-

thing to make the journey back a little easier for Drew than the one here had been.

'I can manage. And I can't believe I'm the one saying this but stay down for the rest of the day.' There was a look of quiet humour in his eyes, and Drew was clearly appreciating the irony.

'People tell you to stay down quite a lot, do they?'

'All the time. I thought I'd try it out on you to see if you like it any better than I do.'

'Actually... I don't mind it.' Being looked after like this was a novel experience.

'I'll give you the full treatment, then.' His lips curved into a delicious smile. If she'd been greeted by that when she's woken up, goodness only knew what might have happened, and Caro thanked her lucky stars that he'd saved it until now.

Phoenix had wandered over, it obviously having occurred to her that something might be happening without her. Caro swung her legs off the sofa, and Drew arranged the throw across them carefully, lifting the puppy up and putting her onto Caro's lap.

'Uh...what am I supposed to do now?' Caro was beginning to wonder exactly what *the full treatment* would entail.

'Same as you do with Clarice...' He shot the words over his shoulder as he walked towards the kitchen.

Presumably that didn't mean tinkering with Phoenix's programming. Caro stroked the little dog, and she started to lick her hand. 'She's not going to bite me, is she?'

'She might give it a go, but it'll only be in play. Don't bite her back.' He grinned, opening the fridge door.

That was all very unpredictable. As was the way that Phoenix snuggled into her lap, looking up at Caro as if she was at the very centre of her world. But it was nice to have someone there who could make her feel that nothing was so urgent that it couldn't wait a little while.

She stroked Phoenix while Drew clattered around in the kitchen, looking up when he walked towards her, carrying two mugs. 'What's this?'

'It's the next stage. Random drinks.' He put the mugs down on the coffee table.

'Hot soup. That's nice.' Caro had rather been hoping for coffee, strong enough to jolt her out of this feeling of delicious laziness.

'Yeah. Nourishing and unlikely to keep you awake.' He lowered himself onto the sofa next to her. 'Now. Afternoon TV. I'm quite an aficionado.'

He reached for the remote, turning on the television that was mounted on the wall in the corner of the room. 'What do you fancy? Home improvements?'

Caro shook her head. You needed to *have* a home in order to improve it. He flipped through the channels, listing the options.

'Or you can have a whodunit... Sherlock Holmes?'

'I don't mind that.'

Drew grinned. 'Perfect. You don't want anything that you like too much in case it encourages you to think.'

'You're enjoying this a bit too much, Drew.'

He chuckled, leaning back against the cushions. 'You have to admit that I'm very good at it, though.'

Yeah. Something told Caro that Drew was good at everything he did. Even the process of letting an afternoon slip by, without having done anything constructive. He'd probably had a little too much of that recently.

She leaned forward to pick up her mug, and Phoenix escaped her lap in favour of Drew's. 'Okay. So when we've done with the hot drinks and the afternoon TV...?'

'I'll go home. You can watch some more TV and then get some sleep.'

'That sounds thrilling. And what about the project?'

'I've got a proposition for you.'

'Sounds exciting.' Damn! That had just slipped out. The proposition was almost certainly work related…

'Wait till you hear it.' Drew took a moment to reach for his own mug and take a sip from it, and Caro wondered if he was trying for a Master of Suspense effect, or if the soup and the TV were having an effect on him also.

'Write a couple of introductory paragraphs about your project. You can be as vague as you like, there's no need to give away anything you don't want anyone to know. I'll append that to an email asking some of our dog owners if they'd like to participate in the initial study.'

'Okay, thanks. I'll do that…' Caro pulled the throw away from her legs. She could apply her mind to that simple task while Sherlock Holmes tackled the more difficult question of tracking down a criminal mastermind.

She felt Drew's hand on her shoulder, and Phoenix scrambled out of the way as he leaned across to arrange the throw across her legs again. 'Tomorrow's soon enough. Are you going to stay put?'

Who in their right mind would want to move now? When he was so close and the bulk of his body, along with the tenderness of his hands, were so very apparent.

'If you insist.'

He smiled. Before Caro could wonder whether his lips were as soft as they looked, he'd moved away.

'Of course I insist. Are you doing anything tomorrow? If you want, we can meet up at the clinic and send out the email. Maybe you could set up your testing equipment and show me what's involved.'

'You're going to help me, then?' Caro hadn't wanted to take his participation for granted.

'Yeah, of course I am. It's an exciting project. I want to see where it goes.'

'Thanks. What time shall I come?'

'Any time after eight?'

'Okay. Eight's fine. I'll be there.'

'Great.' He drained his own mug and picked up hers. It was probably better not to tell him she'd deal with the mugs, and she watched the TV while Drew added them to the rest of the things in the dishwasher and set it running.

'I'll see you tomorrow, then.' He seemed positively breezy now. Moving more easily, even taking a few short steps without his stick. Obviously an afternoon spent sitting down and reading, while she'd slept, had satisfied both his restless mind and his need for physical rest.

'Yeah, okay. You're sure you'll be all right down the steps?'

'Positive.' He called Phoenix and she leapt off the sofa and went careening towards him. He clipped her lead onto her collar and put his coat on, shouldering his canvas bag. 'Watch the TV. And don't sleep in your clothes tonight...'

Caro shot him a look, calculated to imply that sleeping in her clothes was the last thing she'd ever consider doing. Drew chuckled, opening the front door and waiting for Phoenix to follow him through it. Then he was gone.

Now she could stop this game and get on with something. Caro couldn't quite think for the moment exactly what. Maybe she'd just watch through to the end of the film...

Beneath all the playfulness, Drew was obviously frustrated and bored. He still needed some downtime to recuperate from his injuries, but his restless mind also needed

stimulation, and quite by accident she'd managed to contrive both today.

Allowing him to look after her had just been a joke,
but... It had obviously fed a deeper need for Drew. Maybe
a deeper need for her too. No one had ever looked after
her like this.

Not even Blake Harmer. He had been the handsome lec-
turer and she the budding inventor. Ten years older than
her, and touched by the California sun, she'd felt pale and
unworldly next to him, but somehow he'd chosen her. She'd
fallen in love harder and faster than she'd realised was possible, and when he'd asked her to move in with him Caro
had finally found the home that her parents' itinerant life-
style had never given her.

She'd ignored the voices that had whispered behind
their backs, saying she was the more talented of the two.
They hadn't understood.

But then it had become obvious that it was Caro who
didn't understand. The water feature in their garden had
been leaking, and she'd fixed it by making a self-cleaning
valve. By the time she'd realised the potential for its use
in developing countries, Blake had patented it as his own.

She'd hoped it was all a mistake, but had then found
out that the companies Blake had been negotiating with
wouldn't waive their exclusive rights to the new valve for
charitable and non-profit agencies. They'd argued, and
she'd seen the glint of avarice in his eyes.

*'Suck it up, Caro. You can play with your robots and
your wild dreams all you like, someone has to deal with
the money side of things. Since you don't seem capable of
doing that, you should leave it to me...'*

When the news had got out that Blake had lucrative offers for the rights to the valve, and was leaving his teaching
post, the whispers had begun again. What had he seen in

Caro anyway? Had it only been the chance to make money from her inventions? This time Caro believed them. Blake hadn't ever wanted her for herself, just what she could do for him.

She'd run. Put her legal claim against Blake into the hands of an attorney and fled back to England. *This* time her designs would be used for the purpose that she intended. *This* time her heart wouldn't break.

Now she saw things more clearly. Someone like Drew could never find her attractive. He might want to work with her. He might even like her a little. He'd even attempted to address the cost of making her wild dreams work, in effort and time, which was something that Blake had never done. But she shouldn't get carried away and think that there was anything more to it than just an attempt to be nice.

Caro shifted on the sofa, curling up under the throw. She was warm and comfortable, and felt more relaxed than she had in a long time. She could accept that one small favour from Drew, even if she could take nothing else.

CHAPTER FOUR

DREW HADN'T BEEN able to stop thinking about Caro. She was obstinate, entrancing, and he'd never met anyone like her before. Maybe that was it. He'd just never met anyone like her, and she fascinated him.

Fascination wasn't the way to go. Interest would be sufficient. An evening spent thinking about Caro had only confirmed his first impressions. She was talented and beautiful, any man's dream. But she was also a workaholic, and that meant that she couldn't be *his* dream.

But his eagerness to see Caro again had peeled him out of bed early and taken him to the veterinary clinic almost before he'd had a chance to think about how his leg was feeling today. He sat in his office, drafting the email that invited the clinic's dog owners to participate in Caro's study.

His phone rang, and Tegan's voice sounded on the other end of the line. *'Drew...!'*

'Yep...' He wasn't sure who else Tegan might think it was, but since he'd been back, their receptionist had been enunciating his name with an excited emphasis every time he completed the simple task of answering his phone.

'You have a visitor. Ms Barnes is here to see you.'

Tegan made that sound fabulous and exciting too, and Drew resisted the temptation to agree with her.

'Great, thanks, Tegan. I'll be right out.' He hung up before Tegan could volunteer to bring Caro through to his office.

He was halfway along the corridor that led to the reception area when he saw Caro burst through the swing doors at the far end, wheeling an equipment case. Drew was so surprised that he forgot to keep walking...

Her hair shone in the overhead lights, caught back in a complicated plait that seemed to owe something to nature and something else to design. She wore a pair of slim, dark trousers with a red jacket, and the material of her cream blouse looked as if it might be silky to the touch. Caro was immaculate. And...it was so blatantly obvious that he couldn't ignore it...beautiful.

'Good morning.' She stopped in front of him, and he realised that her honey-brown eyes were yet another thing he should have noticed. All part of her softness.

'You made it...' Drew felt suddenly tongue-tied.

'Looks like it.' She gave him a bewitching smile, leaning confidingly towards him, and Drew felt the back of his neck tingle in response to her scent. 'It was the evil stepfather.'

'What...?' Maybe this was one of those confusing non sequiturs that dreams threw up from time to time.

'Sherlock Holmes deduced the answer, though.'

'Oh! That. I was wondering if you'd go straight back to work after I left.'

'No, I stayed on the sofa all afternoon. Did Phoenix make it home all right?'

The mischief in her eyes told him that she was really asking about him. Her concern didn't feel diminishing, though, as if he couldn't manage on his own.

'Yeah. We both rested up yesterday evening.'

He turned, the sound of Caro's dry laughter echoing

in his ears. He could get used to that. Making her laugh a little more and work a little less…

Although today was all about work. Obviously. Why else would they be spending time together?

He led the way to his office, and she parked her case in the corner and sat down. Drew printed out his email and handed it to her, and she read it through, nodding her approval.

'Here's mine.' She pulled a memory stick from her handbag, and Drew plugged it into his laptop.

'It's too long.'

'You haven't even read it yet!' Caro frowned at him, folding her arms in a clear signal that he'd better do so, and that she'd wait while he did. Under her delicious scrutiny, Drew focussed his eyes on the screen.

'This is all interesting.' And his original comment still stood. 'But it's too long. People don't need to wade through all of the reasons that the project's interesting, they just need to know what we're asking of them and the positive good that their participation will do.'

She rolled her eyes. 'You're not one of these people that likes to oversimplify everything, are you?'

Drew pursed his lips. Caro's idea of simple wasn't the same as most other people's. 'I don't fully understand the second paragraph, and I've read your initial specification.'

She frowned, walking around his desk to peer over his shoulder at the screen. As she leaned across, seemingly unaware that her arm was touching his shoulder, he felt the hairs on his forearm raise in response.

'Okay, delete para two. And the third para rather relies on the concepts explained in the second, so you'd better get rid of that as well…'

It didn't take long to distil the description down, but by the time she returned to her seat, Drew's head was spinning. So much for keeping things professional. Maybe if he concentrated on looking and sounding professional, then his instincts would get the idea and follow suit.

'I'll send this through to Tegan, then? She has the mailing list and she'll send the emails out.'

'That's great, thank you.' There was a hint of excitement in Caro's tone. It was the beginning of a new challenge, and suddenly it all seemed new and exciting to Drew, too.

He led her through to his consulting room, showing her where she could set up her camera and the force plates that would measure the animal's gait and the force generated by each foot strike. Caro looked around the room thoughtfully.

'I want to quantify climbing movements as well...'

'We have a set of steps that will help with that. Lucas is going to bring them from the storeroom when he's finished his morning surgery.' Drew's phone rang and he answered it.

He knew that Caspian Smythe-Bingham always kept his phone handy to respond to emails and social media, but he hadn't expected him to be this quick. Or this positive. Drew smiled, asking him to hold on for a moment.

'We have our first participant. Caspian can bring his Pekingese in any time this week. When are you free?'

'Tomorrow!' Caro's enthusiasm sent a tingle racing down Drew's spine. 'Or any time this week. Whenever suits you.'

Drew smiled, speaking into the phone. 'How would tomorrow at ten suit you, Caspian?'

The date was set, and Caro was finding it difficult to conceal her excitement.

'So we're ready to start. I'll have to calibrate my equipment, I don't suppose you have a dog with nothing to do right now, do you?' She made it sound like a wonderful adventure that was just waiting for them to plunge in.

'I'll ask Ellie if we can borrow her Labrador for a few hours.' He laughed at Caro's sudden expression of dismay. 'Esmerelda is Phoenix's mother. And she's very placid, she won't eat you.'

'I'll take your word for it.' Caro was obviously willing to negotiate any danger to push her project forward. She unbuttoned the sleeves of her blouse, rolling them up. The perfect, pristine version of Caro was beginning to give way to the mussed-up work version, and Drew wondered which he liked the most.

Both. He liked them both.

Caro had always been of the opinion that you didn't actually have to *like* anyone or anything in order to invent something. Sure, you had to know a bit, so that the work was appropriate and solved a problem. But treating every dog that came into the surgery as if it were a long-lost uncle or auntie wasn't necessary.

She supposed it was necessary for Drew. He must like animals, otherwise he wouldn't have become a vet. They had ten people on the list to be seen today, and Drew's manner with each of the dogs calmed them so that it was easier to put them through the various exercises that Caro had devised. There was a different side of Drew to see each time. Man and dog. Handsome man and puppy. Smiling, disastrously attractive man, taming a troublesome Pekingese. And so it went…

'Peter…' He smiled broadly at the young lad who entered the consulting room with his mother and a brown and white puppy. 'Thank you for bringing Rolf along…'

'How are you, Drew?' Peter's mother asked the inevitable question. Everyone seemed to know Drew, and they were all concerned about him.

'I'm good, thanks, Laura.' Drew's smile didn't betray

the fact that this had already been asked and answered more times than Caro cared to count this morning. 'Very happy to be back at work. How's Brian? I haven't seen him in a while.'

'Oh, fine. Pretty busy at work. Everyone's car seems to have something wrong with it at the moment...' Laura's hand flew to her mouth. 'Sorry...'

Drew grinned, shrugging off the gaffe, and bent down towards Rolf. The pup nuzzled at his outstretched hand, seeing only a new friend.

'This is Caro. You've seen the information about her research? Do you have any questions?' Drew introduced her in much the same way he'd done before, and Caro smiled at Laura.

'We'll leave the details to you, Drew. We're happy just to participate.' Laura smiled back, eying the camera and the force plates. It had already occurred to Caro that most of the people they'd seen this morning were here because they liked and trusted Drew.

'Do you want to film us?' Peter looked up enquiringly at Caro, and she was about to show him how the treadmill worked when Drew broke in.

'Yes, that would be great. Perhaps we could just walk Rolf up and down over there for starters.' Drew pointed to a space to one side of the area that had been set aside for filming.

Caro flashed him a questioning look and Drew gave a small nod. If that was the way he wanted things...

They'd said that they would be filming, and Caro supposed she'd better do so, even if this wasn't one of the exercises that all of the other dogs had done. She disengaged the camera from the treadmill, switching it on as Peter walked Rolf up and down. Drew was concentrating hard on the puppy, and Caro thought she saw concern on his face.

There was something he wasn't saying. Peter had obviously already given his heart to his puppy, and the thought that there might be something wrong with him tore at Caro. Drew seemed intent on watching the way that the puppy moved, and she asked Peter to walk him up and down a few times more.

'Okay, that's good.' Drew shot her a smile. Please... *please*...let that be a good sign. Maybe he'd decided he was mistaken in whatever he thought he'd seen. But when he gently lifted the puppy up onto the examination table, Caro saw an extra tenderness in the way Drew gently stroked him and knew that everything *wasn't* all right.

'I think we should take an X-ray, Laura.' Drew spoke quietly, and Laura nodded. She'd seen the way that Drew had carefully examined the puppy's back, legs and hips.

But Peter hadn't and Caro could practically see the questions forming in the boy's eyes. If she couldn't help with the puppy, this was something she could help with.

'Hey, Peter, I'd like to give you a little thank-you for helping with my research.' She reached into her bag and the boy's head turned, his attention drawn away from what Drew was doing.

She'd used the 3D printer to make a few small carapaces, equipped them with sensors and circuitry, and put them into her bag. As she drew the model of the tiny tortoise out of her bag, Peter's eyes widened, in just the way she'd hoped.

'What is it?'

'There's a little switch underneath, just push that...' When Peter pressed his fingers on the spot she'd indicated, the tortoise's legs started to work. 'Now put him down onto the floor.'

Peter started to cackle with glee as the tiny tortoise began to scurry across the floor. When Caro put her foot in its path, he caught his breath as the tortoise swerved out of the way, avoiding the obstacle and making its way towards Drew.

He reached for his stick, planting the end in front of the tortoise until it had turned full circle to make its way back towards Peter. The boy caught it up, turning it over in his hands.

'Can it see me?' Peter was staring intently at the tiny head.

Caro was about to explain that the tortoise couldn't actually *see* anything, and that the sensors simply registered any obstacle that was placed in its path. But Drew had a different answer.

'I think he's taking a look at you right now.'

That satisfied Peter. He put the tortoise back down onto the floor, running to place his foot in its path, and beaming when it swerved out of the way.

There was something in Drew's eyes. He knew that she was trying to divert Peter's attention. 'Why don't you and Caro go and show it to Tegan, while your mum and I finish off the research with Rolf?'

'That's a wonderful idea.' Laura beamed suddenly. 'Thank you so much, Caro.'

'We'll bring one along for Tegan, shall we?' Caro reached into her bag, taking out two more of the tortoises. Putting them on a tabletop, and watching them avoid the edges of the table and each other would keep Peter occupied while Drew did whatever it was he needed to do for Rolf.

The plan worked. Peter followed Caro out into the reception area, and Tegan let out a little scream of excitement when he showed her the tortoise. When Caro handed her one, she planted a red lipstick kiss on its carapace, and walked over to the coffee table, clearing it of magazines.

'Tortoise wars, eh, Peter?' Tegan knelt down on the floor at one end of the table and motioned for Peter to sit at the other end. The phone rang, and Tegan ignored it completely in favour of watching the two tortoises swerve to avoid each other, so Caro leaned over the reception desk to answer it.

'Oh… Um… Hang on a moment, please…' She saw Lucas, looking around for his next patient, and beckoned him over. 'Someone would like an appointment…'

'Okay, thanks.' Lucas took the phone, tapping on Tegan's computer to make the appointment, and then bidding the caller a cheery goodbye. Then he turned to Caro, frowning, as Tegan shrieked with laughter.

'What's going on?'

'Don't disturb them. Drew's taken Peter's puppy to be X-rayed and… I think there's something wrong with it.' Caro shrugged miserably. 'I don't know what, but he seemed pretty keen on keeping Peter occupied with something else.'

Understanding dawned in Lucas's eyes. 'I see. I'll stay and answer the phone, then. My next patient isn't here yet.'

'That's okay, I can do that. I'll take messages and Tegan can phone everyone back.' Caro slipped behind the reception desk, sitting down and taking the last tortoise from her pocket. Wordlessly she handed it to Lucas.

He found the switch and grinned when the little legs began to move. 'That's very cool.'

It seemed that tortoises had the ability to take everyone's mind off the one thing that was consuming her thoughts. What if Drew found something seriously wrong with the puppy? How would Peter react then?

'I hope…' She was desperate for the reassurance that she knew Lucas wasn't in a position to give. Lucas looked up at her suddenly.

'Drew's the best at what he does.' His quiet words slowed the thump of Caro's heart.

'Not you?' She managed a smile.

'I'm the best when he's not around. You're sure you'll be okay here for a minute?'

'I'll be fine. Go…' Lucas would be able to reassure Peter better than she could if he decided to question what was going on with his puppy.

'All right. Call me if you need me. And thank you, Caro.'

'My pleasure.'

Caro watched as Lucas walked over to the coffee table, motioning to Tegan to sit back down again when she saw him and jumped to her feet. Peter chuckled with glee as the three tiny tortoises wove around each other on the table-top. Now all she had to do was sit and wait and hope that Rolf was going to be all right.

Drew had explained everything to Laura, and when he made his way back to the reception desk he found Caro answering the phone, while everyone else was crowded around the coffee table. She seemed very alone, and the agonised look she gave him after he'd dragged Peter away and sent him on his way with his mother tore at his heart.

'They are such fun!' Tegan bounced back to the reception desk, handing her tortoise back to Caro with a hint of reluctance. Caro found a smile from somewhere.

'Keep it, if you like.'

'Can I? Thank you! I can paint its shell…' Tegan displayed her purple sparkly nails, in an indication of how her tortoise might look like when she'd finished with it. 'I'll put it on the table and the kids will love playing with it.'

'Perhaps we can commission some from you, Caro?'

Drew wasn't sure whether Caro knew just how much she'd helped by keeping Peter entertained.

'Great idea. How much are they?' Lucas asked.

Caro shrugged. 'They don't cost anything much to print, and the micro-electrics are pretty standard. I'd be happy to make some more for you.'

Lucas looked as if he was about to protest, and Drew silenced him with a shake of his head. They could sort all that out later, and he'd make sure that Caro was recompensed for her work, even if they just bought new supplies for her 3D printer. Caro obviously had something more important on her mind, and that meant that Drew did too. He hurried her away and back to the consulting room.

'What's the matter with Rolf?' The question came almost as soon as he'd closed the door behind them.

'First things first. He's going to be all right.'

'Oh! Thank goodness.' Caro flopped down into a chair. 'I should have known, really. Lucas said you were the best at what you do...'

Warmth flowed through Drew's veins. Not just because Lucas had said it but because Caro had heard it. 'I'm the best when he's not around.'

'He said the same about you.' Caro smiled suddenly. 'What about Ellie?'

Drew chuckled. 'Ellie's in a league all of her own. Neither Lucas nor I presume to compete with that.'

She nodded. 'Wise move. So what did you see, Drew? Something to do with Rolf's gait?'

She was perceptive, noticing everything. That was probably one of the things that made Caro so good at what she did. Along with a liberal helping of hard work, which Drew preferred not to think about at the moment, because it always prompted a flutter of concern for her in his heart.

'Yes, I noticed that he's got a slightly swaying gait, which is one of the signs of canine hip dysplasia.'

Caro's eyes widened in alarm. 'I don't know what that is...'

Drew sat down opposite her. 'It's quite a common genetic condition, where the hip develops laxity early in a puppy's development. If left unchecked, it can cause a great deal of pain and stiffness, but we've caught it early so there's lots we can do to prevent it from developing. I think that Rolf will be able to live a perfectly happy and pain-free life.'

She nodded, clasping her hands together. 'That's...good. What are you going to do?'

Caro needed all the information she could get so that she could fit all the pieces of the puzzle together. Drew smiled. He was beginning to like the way that her mind worked.

He got to his feet, fetching the model of a canine hip from the glass-doored cabinet, and when he turned he found her standing at his elbow. 'Okay, here's how it works. In the first few weeks of a puppy's life the ligaments that stabilise the joint can become loose, eroding the cartilage so that the bone doesn't develop properly. When the puppy moves, the joint is displaced, like this...'

Caro winced as he demonstrated. 'That looks...horrible.'

'If it's allowed to develop it can be. But I've given Laura an exercise and feeding programme for Rolf that will help stabilise these joints, and I'll be checking on him regularly. That'll mean he doesn't develop all of the secondary wear and tear that will start to cause him pain.'

'He's not in pain now?'

'No, he isn't.'

A tear suddenly rolled down Caro's cheek. For all her insistence on the science, she had a soft heart that was just as beautiful as her mind. Drew wanted to hug her but didn't dare, telling himself that this wasn't the right place. In truth, nowhere was ever going to be the right place, because he knew that hugging Caro would reach parts of his own heart that were forbidden.

Instead, he handed her the model of the joint. She nodded, trying the movements for herself, and then seemed to notice the tear, which was now travelling across her chin, and brushed it away impatiently. If hugging her was a step too far, then Drew supposed that kissing the tear away was a giant leap across the boundaries that he'd imposed on himself.

'Thank you for looking after Peter. It was a great help, and he didn't need to know that I was concerned. Laura will explain everything to him when they get home, and she'll be able to tell him the same as I've told you, that Rolf will be all right.'

'It was…nothing.' Caro shrugged. 'I couldn't bear to think that he might be worried about his puppy.'

'It was everything…' A lump blocked Drew's throat. He took the model from Caro's hands, putting it back into the cabinet, and turned away. Whatever he did next, he had to keep his distance to avoid anything that had even the slightest chance of turning physical.

'Would a wire-frame model help to isolate the differences in movement?' Her mind was obviously starting to work, embracing all the possibilities. 'I expect that's already been done…'

'There are a lot of studies on canine hip dysplasia, and since early diagnosis is so important many of them concentrate on how to diagnose accurately. I can get some of the literature for you if you're interested.' He lowered himself into a chair.

'Yes, I'm interested. I probably wouldn't be able to contribute anything, but you never know…'

Drew knew. Caro had a way of stripping a problem down and seeing it in many different ways, and if she set her mind to it he'd be surprised if she couldn't add a little something to the sum total of knowledge on any subject.

'You're not going to get diverted from the prosthetics project, are you?'

She grinned suddenly, rubbing one hand in a circle over her stomach and using the other to tap her head in an impressive show of co-ordination. 'I can do more than one thing at a time.'

'Right, then.' Drew ignored the hard spike of desire that shot through him. Finding out how many things Caro could do at one time, and then concentrating her mind on just one, over-arching sensation was an entirely inappropriate thought, and there wasn't a situation that was going to change that. He seriously needed to get a grip.

'So… Are you ready for our next visitor?'

'I need to take a break.'

The words were surprisingly easy to say, even if they did prompt a grimace of disappointment from Caro. In the three hours since they'd started work, her manner had changed a little, her quiet wariness of their canine test subjects beginning to dissolve. She'd even stroked a particularly docile spaniel without glancing at Drew first for reassurance, and Drew had fought to hide a smile.

But now he was tired. His leg was beginning to ache, and he knew that he'd reach a point soon where he would *have* to sit down.

'Lucas is still doing his morning surgery, and if you wanted to join him, I'm sure he wouldn't mind. Perhaps he could send some of his patients your way for the study.'

She raised her eyebrows, as if he'd suggested something

that was beyond outrageous. A little stir of gratification nudged at Drew's heart.

'No, that's okay. I think I have what I need for this morning. Anyway, I've trained *you* up now.'

Drew chuckled. He was finding it more and more difficult to resist Caro's forthright manner and the way that she reddened slightly when she realised that she'd said what was on her mind without applying the usual filters.

'Glad to hear it. I'll try and remember the drill for the next time.'

'Good. Shall I go and get us some lunch from the cafeteria?'

He'd really like to stroll over there with her and get his own lunch. But something about Caro always made him feel stronger and more useful than he usually did these days, and it didn't seem quite so galling to let go of the reins from time to time.

'A ham and cheese toastie, if they have one, and some coffee. Put it all on my account.'

'Okay. Lunch is on you, then, thank you.' Caro made it sound as if he'd just asked her to dine at an exclusive restaurant. But in truth nothing was more luxurious than the chance to just watch her as she crossed the room, the overhead lights teasing the shine from her hair.

CHAPTER FIVE

CARO COULD GET used to ham and cheese toasties. These weren't as tasty as the ones that Drew had made, but she was a great deal more awake to appreciate them. They'd gone to his office to eat, and the ashen tiredness in his face had begun to lift a little. He'd stayed put while she'd taken her laptop from her bag, opening it on his desk and scanning through the data from the force plates.

'You have what you need? Or are you still at the stage where vets shouldn't interfere with your process?' There was a sudden tension in his voice that told Caro he was expecting an answer that he didn't want to hear. A week ago, he probably would have got it, but now... She'd seen Drew work, and he was truly dedicated to the welfare of the animals under his care. Caro didn't feel the same need to keep him at arm's length.

'No. Vets are very welcome to interfere with my process at the moment.' *One* vet. Carol liked Lucas and Ellie, and she was sure that they were both completely trustworthy. But Drew was the vet she was beginning to actually trust.

'That's reassuring. I wouldn't want to meddle.'

She supposed she'd asked for that one, making him sign the non-disclosure agreement. But since she had, perhaps it was okay to share a little. However risky her heart told her it was.

'I don't suppose you'd mind taking a look through these results, would you? I can analyse the data from a mechanics point of view, but it would be good to get another perspective.'

He looked pleased. A little surprised as well. 'Yeah, sure, I'd be happy to. I'll come to you and we can review them together?'

'Yes. Thanks.'

Nice. It felt nice to have someone to share her ideas with. The taste of danger in the thought only seemed to add a bit of extra spice. Maybe that was what had been missing from her work in the last few months. The sense of reaching out into the unknown that drove her forward.

'I know that the people who came today did so because *you* asked them. I really appreciate that. They're all very kind…'

Perhaps *too* kind. Everyone seemed to be so careful around him, and it clearly made Drew uneasy. But Caro shouldn't say it, Blake had told her more than once that voicing whatever was on her mind wasn't her most attractive trait.

He was looking at her questioningly. 'Don't let me down now, Caro. I was starting to appreciate your habit of saying exactly what you mean.'

'I just… I was wondering if this "*poor Drew*" thing that everyone seems to have is helping. It's not my business…'

He let out a short, barking laugh. 'One of the things about living in a village is that everyone knows your business. I don't see why you should be any different.'

Caro took a deep breath. '*Is* it helping, then?'

'Everyone's been really supportive, and I appreciate it more than I can say. And, no, it's not helping. I feel as if no one has any expectations of me any more.' He smiled suddenly. 'Apart from you, of course.'

'Is there anything else I should know? That might make me rethink my expectations?' If he wanted honesty then Caro was up for that. It saved a lot of time and beating around the bush.

'You don't need to rethink anything.' He narrowed his eyes, searching her face, and it occurred to Caro that she wasn't the only one who had reason to be cautious. 'Two years ago I lost my fiancée in a diving accident.'

'I'm sorry. You've had a lot of hurt to bear in a very short time.' Caro's own troubles seemed insignificant in the face of this.

'It doesn't define me.' There was a trace of defiance in his tone.

She didn't know what to say to him. And then it occurred to Caro that this was Drew's problem. Everyone knew what had happened and no one talked about it.

'Were you there? When your fiancée died?'

Something ignited in his eyes. An understanding between them that it was okay to ask, because Drew wanted to answer.

'No. Luna and I had a shared interest in marine conservation, that's how we met. She was a member of a team that travelled a lot and I was busy here, building up the practice with Ellie.'

'So you didn't get to see her as much as you wanted?'

Drew puffed out a sigh. 'Luna was very determined, and I always knew she'd stop at nothing for the things she believed in. It was one of the things I loved about her. She'd driven for two days to get to the team's encampment, and she was exhausted, but she went diving anyway.'

A prickle of embarrassment travelled down Caro's spine. She was no stranger to working for two days straight and fighting exhaustion to do just that bit more. Drew's insistence on food and afternoon TV the other day hadn't been a whim.

'And you think that if you'd been there, you might have stopped her?' Caro shook her head. It was a natural enough reaction, but it could only lead to more grief.

He shrugged. 'I can't say that the thought didn't occur to me. But I couldn't have stopped her from taking risks. That was in her nature and you can't change the people you love.'

'You reckon not?' Blake should have taken note of that. He'd spent an appreciable amount of time suggesting clothes that would suit her and pointing out what she shouldn't say or do. It had all been a terrible waste, though, because he hadn't really wanted her because she was beautiful or charming. She had just been someone who had ideas that could be turned into hard cash.

'I'm not sure I could ever change who I am. Could you?'

Caro swallowed hard. 'No. I don't think so.' It seemed like an admission of failure. Drew made her wish that she *was* beautiful and charming.

'I guess we'll just have to be what we are...' He quirked his lips downwards as if he didn't really want to think about that. 'Would you like to come for a walk? We have a beach, and some woodlands...'

Suddenly she didn't want to be near Drew any more. He'd never once criticised her, but she couldn't stop the things that Blake had said from echoing in her mind.

'No, thanks, but... I should be getting back. The tide...'

'Yes, of course. I'm running late too, I'll have to hurry home if I'm going to catch the last of this afternoon's TV.'

Caro breathed a sigh of relief. She'd be home soon, in her workshop, where she didn't have to think about any of this. 'I'm told it does you a lot of good.'

'Whoever told you that?' Drew smirked at her, getting to his feet.

* * *

What? What had that all been about? Drew let himself into his cottage on the outskirts of the tiny village of Dolphin Cove, scarcely having time for the thought before Phoenix came hurtling towards him.

'Hey, there, girl.' He bent down to stroke the puppy, lifting her up into his arms. 'You missed me, then?'

The answer was unequivocal. Phoenix started to lick his neck, and Drew couldn't help smiling. She was the most uncomplicated part of his life at the moment.

Caro, on the other hand…

He'd known her for two days. And found himself spilling things he'd kept from people he'd known his whole life. It was puzzling, and a little outrageous, and maybe just the result of her blunt honesty. But he couldn't shake the feeling that Caro somehow got him in a way that most other people didn't.

It was almost as if she knew him, right down to his bones, the way that Ellie did. But Ellie's knowing was the result of them having grown up with each other. Brother and sister. Caro's knowing was warm and wild and confronting, and he couldn't seem to get enough of it. It had followed him home, digging into his heart, like a sharp longing for what he couldn't have.

And he *couldn't* have it. He couldn't change Caro, any more than he could have changed Luna. His parents had argued their way through his teens, both trying to change each other. The divorce had been a long time coming, postponed until he and his brothers had all left home, and it had probably been the best thing that had ever happened to his parents. Finally, they'd learned how to be friends, and they got on together much better than when they'd been married.

Man's best friend was still making an excited fuss of

him. He scratched behind Phoenix's ears, and the puppy wriggled with pleasure.

'Sorry to leave you for so long. When you've had your final round of shots, you can come to the clinic while I'm working.'

Phoenix didn't seem to care about anything other than this moment, she was just happy that he was home now. And maybe looking just a few moments ahead, in anticipation of some dog treats. He set her down, and she trotted ahead of him as he made his way into the kitchen.

Caro had been staring at her computer screen for two hours, ever since Drew had replied to her text, confirming that he'd be coming to see her later on today. He'd clearly forgotten all about the tide, because he'd said he'd be there at noon, and he'd replied to Caro's reminder with a thumbs-up emoji. Whatever that meant. Thumbs up for the tide? Or for not arriving until later in the afternoon?

In the meantime, though, she was safe from visitors. That was the whole point of living up here, but at the moment it seemed an annoyance. She stared out of the window of her workshop at the sea, following the movement of a small rowing boat that was making its way around the peninsula.

Whoever that was must be mad. Wherever they needed to get to it couldn't be more than five minutes' drive, and pitching yourself out into the water just for the sake of it seemed perverse. Maybe she should go outside, just to make sure that the small craft didn't capsize while it was traversing her small slice of the horizon.

She may as well. She wasn't getting anything done here, and perhaps the breeze that continually danced across her small island would clear her head a little. Caro pulled on the sweater that was draped over the back of her chair and squeezed past the printer, unlocking the door.

Whoever it was was pulling strongly on the oars. Caro narrowed her eyes at the splash of red at the prow of the boat. Was it two people…?

She let out a little yelp of surprise. It was a small dog, wearing a bright red lifejacket. And the man pulling at the oars was Drew.

That put a different complexion on the whole thing. Now the raw power in his shoulders made her heart beat a little faster. And the desperate foolhardiness of the venture became a little more personal. Caro ran to the edge of the cliff that dropped down towards the sea and shouted.

'Drew… Drew!'

He didn't hear her the first time, but when she screamed at the top of her voice, he stopped rowing, grinning up at her. That wasn't what she'd meant him to do. He should be heading for the beach, where he'd be safe.

'What are you doing? Be careful!'

He seemed to be allowing the tide to bring him closer to the foot of the cliff.

Drew swung one of the oars into the boat and waved at her. He was just twenty feet below her now, the boat bobbing up and down on the water, and he seemed to be looking for something. Then he reached forward, pulling the boat right up against the rocks.

'I said I'd be here at twelve.' He looked up at her, his face all innocence. He could cut that out right now.

'I didn't expect you to row here. What are you going to do now?' The cliff face that separated them was a sheer expanse of rock. No one could get up it, and certainly not a man with an injured leg and a puppy to contend with.

'Have you been down into your basement?'

'Only once.' The agent had insisted on showing her the

whole of the house, but the dark, empty space hadn't much appealed to Caro.

'I'll meet you there.'

'What?'

Too late. The boat had disappeared into a crevice and taken Drew and Phoenix with it. She could hear the puppy's excited barking, but short of throwing herself into the sea there was no way of seeing what Drew was up to now. Caro wrapped her arms around her, tramping back to the house.

The door into the basement was locked, and she twisted the key, switching on the light and walking down the stone steps. What was she supposed to do now? Caro looked around and caught sight of a new-looking door at the far end of the space.

That too was locked, but the key was in the lock and the mechanism turned smoothly when she tried it. The door swung open, and she saw Drew, walking towards her with a torch in one hand and Phoenix's lead in the other. The puppy seemed to be having a fine old time, still wearing her lifejacket and yelping excitedly.

Drew grinned at her. His shoulders seemed somehow broader now that she'd seen them powering the fragile craft through the waves towards her, and he looked deliciously windswept. That was something she could think about later, when she'd questioned the advisability of arriving this way.

'What do you think you're doing, Drew? Couldn't you just wait for the tide?'

He shrugged. 'Rowing's a lot easier than climbing steps.'

'And it's a lot more dangerous as well. Goodness only knows what might have happened to you. And Phoenix.'

If he had little heed for his own safety, then she knew that he'd baulk over having put Phoenix at risk.

'It's an easy row, around from Dolphin Cove. If it was dangerous I wouldn't have come this way, but it's a nice day and these waters are sheltered enough. I've been rowing back and forth in them since I was a kid.'

'You're a *vet,* Drew. Not a crusty old fisherman.'

He chuckled. 'True. But my grandfather's a crusty old fisherman, and he was the one who taught me how to row and showed me every inch of this coastline.'

Caro puffed out a breath. 'All right, then. I still don't like it.'

'What on earth did you do when you were in California? I hear there's a great deal of sea there.'

'They call it ocean. And, yes, there is, but…' She shrugged awkwardly.

'You were a bit busy with other things?'

'Yes, as it happens, I was.' Caro peered past him into the darkness. 'What is this, some kind of secret passage?'

'It's an open secret, most people around here know about it.' He turned, beckoning her into the gloomy space.

When her eyes adjusted to the darkness, Caro could see that it was more of a cavern than a passage. She could hear the sound of the sea and see light at the other end.

'So this is a landing? For any visitors who can't be bothered to climb the steps?' The small wooden rowing boat was pulled up out of the water, inside the mouth of the opening onto the sea.

'You really don't know? What's this place called?'

Ah. Smugglers' Top. 'This is an old smuggling route?'

'That's the story. I don't know whether it's true or not, but why else would anyone go to the trouble of opening up this cavern? It's big enough to land any amount of contraband, and it would be pretty difficult for the excise to lie in wait and capture you here.'

'What do you do with it once you've got it here, though?' Caro looked around the cavern, half expecting to find a long-abandoned crate of brandy in one of the corners.

'I suppose you could bring it down onto the beach when you know it's safe. Or take it along the coast by sea.' Drew shrugged. 'It's just an old story.'

'And how did you know that the passage hadn't been filled in, when they renovated the house?'

'I gave Stella a call, at the letting agents. She told me that it was still okay to land here, and that they'd just put a lock on the cellar door so that no one could get through into the house.' He grinned. 'I think she must have mentioned it when she showed you around.'

The perils of a small village. And not listening to everything that the letting agent had had to say. Caro had switched off when Stella had launched into yet another story about the history around here.

'And so you decided to do it the traditional way. In a wooden boat.' Phoenix clearly approved of the craft as she was pawing at the side of it, wanting to get back in.

'What's wrong with that?' Drew raised his eyebrows.

'Nothing, I suppose. Only a motor would have been easier. Along with something to help you steer.'

'You steer with your oar strokes. And in a small boat like this, an outboard motor doesn't let you feel way the tide's running.'

Of course. How come she didn't know that?

It was because they were so different. Caro worked with absolutes, data and programming, robots that would react according to a set range of values. Drew relied on his senses to deal with the unpredictable behaviour of the world around him. How two people with such different approaches could understand each other so well was one of those imponderable questions that had a habit of keeping Caro awake at night.

'*You* can feel it. I'd be over the side as soon as a wave hit me.' She grinned up at him.

'Nah. You'd invent something and fly over the tops of the waves.'

'Probably. You want to come upstairs for some rum and hard tack?'

He chuckled. 'You got me hard tack? How did you know that was my favourite?'

CHAPTER SIX

THEY'D WORKED FOR a full five hours, trading ideas over a steady stream of snacks from the kitchen. Drew had enjoyed himself, and when the time came for him to row the boat back to Dolphin Cove, he felt his body thrumming with strength. His leg still hurt a little, but he was nine tenths alive now, instead of feeling half-dead.

Phoenix tugged at her lead when she saw the boat, eager to resume her position at the prow. Most dogs liked the water but, much to his grandfather's delight, Phoenix was turning into a real sailor.

'Will you be all right?' Caro stared out at the sea, as if it really did conceal monsters.

'Yeah, we'll be fine.' She didn't seem particularly reassured, and Drew tried again. 'Think of it this way. I've been messing around in boats all my life, and so far it's proved less injurious to my health than driving.'

Drew smiled. He could practically see the cogs turning in her head, weighing up probabilities and risk. Then Caro shook her head, as if the equation was too complex for her.

'I wouldn't know about that. I've never messed about in boats, so I don't have the data.'

An idea sprang into Drew's head. Probably not a good one, but it was enticing, like a siren's call, and he couldn't resist it.

'Would you like to come out for a trip on my dad's boat? We could go one weekend.'

She was turning the idea over in her head. Work or a boat trip. Drew knew how strongly work pulled at her, but Caro was interested in everything, and a new experience was difficult for her to resist as well.

'Can you swim?'

'Yes, I'm a good swimmer…when I'm in the swimming pool, that is. Why, were you thinking of pushing me overboard?'

'Only if you disobey the captain's orders.' Drew chuckled as Caro shot him an exasperated look. 'We can borrow a wetsuit from the diving centre, and if the weather's good I'll show you how to snorkel. There are lots of things going on down there that you've never imagined…'

He was deliberately pushing all of Caro's buttons. The idea of things going on that she couldn't imagine was irresistible to her. Drew had done plenty of swimming and water exercises as part of his rehab, but he hadn't been in the sea since his accident. It was about time he reacquainted himself with the capricious mistress that he'd loved ever since he could walk.

'I'd like that. Can we go down deep?'

He should have known that Caro didn't do anything by halves. 'Not unless you can hold your breath for half an hour. You want to scuba dive?'

She shifted awkwardly from one foot to the other. 'I don't know…'

Drew wasn't quite sure about that either. Since Luna had died, he'd judiciously avoided being responsible for anyone while diving, and had given up his teaching sessions at the diving centre. Maybe it was about time he reacquainted himself with that part of his life, too.

'I'll tell you what. We'll pop down to the centre tomorrow and sign you up for some lessons. They do short courses that last a week and just teach you the basics. If you like it, then you can come out with us the Saturday after next.'

Caro thought for a moment. 'Okay. Thanks. I'll see what's involved tomorrow, and I might just do that.'

Drew nodded. He'd tempted Caro into this, but now that it was a reality his throat seemed a little dry. Maybe he'd prefer it after all if she stayed safely on the boat, but now that Caro had the idea in her head there wasn't going to be any stopping her.

'All right. One thing, though…'

'Yes?' She tipped her head up towards him, and in the shade of the cavern, her eyes seemed to glisten, full of unknown possibilities.

'If you've been up all night, working, you don't get to dive. Ever. Safety's always the number one consideration.'

He heard the sudden blunt assertiveness in his own tone and saw Caro's face soften. Maybe she understood… Drew fought back the temptation to smile. She *needed* to understand this.

'Okay, I hear you. No going into the water unless I've had a solid night's sleep. I promise.'

'Thanks.' Drew could smile now. And that brought with it a new temptation, to kiss her goodbye. It seemed that there was no getting away from wanting just that little bit more with Caro. 'I'll see you tomorrow?'

'Yes.' She bent down, giving Phoenix a hug and a kiss. 'Safe journey back, sweetie. Perhaps you can persuade the old grouch to send me a text when you get home.'

'I'll remind her to remind me.' Drew pushed the small craft down into the water and then stepped into it. Now that his legs didn't need to hold him up, he felt strong again.

And if he needed to be a grouch to keep Caro safe, he'd had plenty of practice over the last few months.

She stood watching them as he manoeuvred the boat around and started to row. Ten yards. Twenty… Her figure was becoming smaller, standing in the mouth of the cavern like a sweet, golden-haired lover, standing at the water's edge to watch the boats go out. His grandfather had told him that his grandmother had done that every time when he put to sea, and Drew had never really understood the impact of the statement.

Then she waved. Drew raised his hand in reply, and then started to row again, pulling hard on the oars. *He* was the one who needed a good night's sleep, to regain some much-needed perspective.

Caro had decided not to mention diving to Drew. She'd been carried away by the thought of exploring new worlds with him, and she'd probably gone too far. His attitude had become suddenly authoritative, and Caro had been re-minded that Drew had conflicting feelings about the sea, and diving in particular. He clearly loved both, but they'd taken his fiancée from him.

This morning it was as if he'd pushed their conversation of last night to the back of his mind and was pretending that it had never happened. That was fair enough. Caro was disappointed, she'd gone to sleep last night thinking about drifting mermaid-like under the sea, finding new and unimagined wonders. But she'd do it with someone else, in another place. There would always be new places, and Drew's peace of mind was far more important.

'So.' They'd eaten their lunch and he leaned back in his seat. 'Are you still up for the diving centre this afternoon?'

'Yes!' She couldn't help replying too quickly and maybe a little too enthusiastically. 'If you are, that is.'

He gave her that gorgeous lazy grin of his. The one that said he'd finished work now, and he was going with the flow. He had a built-in off switch that he seemed to be able to flip at will, and Caro wondered what that might be like.

'Yes, I'm up for it. I'm looking forward to getting back to diving.'

That was that, then. There was no resisting him now, no telling herself that Drew probably wasn't ready for this. He wanted to do it and holding him back was the one thing that Drew really didn't need at the moment.

'Okay. Where's the diving centre?'

'Down there.' He jerked his thumb towards the window, and Caro saw a low, stone building, nestling in the sheltered curve of the beach next to a small jetty.

'There's a diving centre here? Is there anything that you *don't* have?'

Drew grinned. 'Ellie and I developed this place as a resource for the community and a learning centre for all aspects of the natural world.'

'How do you manage it all?' She peered at Drew. 'You don't have an old treasure chest under your bed, do you? Or a rich uncle…?'

'No, nothing like that. We were given the land by a local benefactor, and we've had grants to help develop some of the community and learning aspects of the centre. Ellie and I have been in practice together ever since veterinary school, and when we got the opportunity to expand we grabbed it.'

'So you do diving…and conservation…?'

'Hasn't Lucas shown you around?'

Caro shrugged. 'He gave it a go. I was concentrating on my stuff, and he had stuff with Ellie to think about. Between us, there wasn't a great deal of time for anything other than what was strictly necessary.'

Drew chuckled. 'You think you can tear your head away from your work for a few hours?'

Yes, actually she could. Drew's ability to tear her head away from almost anything was a little frightening, and if Caro wasn't careful, she'd lose focus. But she could worry about that tomorrow, when the sun wasn't shining and his smile wasn't so close at hand.

'I've got a small window of opportunity.'

'I won't let it go to waste, then. I'll give you the guided tour, and then we'll go and see Jake at the diving centre. He's probably having lunch at the moment.'

She followed Drew through the reception area, giving Tegan a wave as they passed. He made for the trees, walking along a woodland path until they were out of earshot of the clinic car park. Leaves were beginning to carpet the ground, and there seemed to be all kinds of rustling going on but Caro couldn't see where it was coming from. Drew sat down on a bench.

'What's here?'

He smiled. 'Wait and see...'

She sat next to him, suppressing the urge to tap her foot. Drew stretched his legs out in front of him, seeming wholly at peace.

Silence. Nothing was happening, and Caro wondered how long they would have to wait before Drew either gave up or they saw something. And then, suddenly, the empty woods began to come to life.

A small pinkish brown bird, with a black beak and bright blue flashes on its wings, seemed to be foraging amongst the undergrowth. Drew leaned over, whispering.

'It's a jay. Looking for acorns to bury for the winter.'

Caro watched the bird as it made its way amongst the fallen leaves, moving them to one side with its beak. Sliding towards him on the bench seemed very natural. They *were* whispering after all…

'Do they remember where they've put them?'

'Often enough, I guess. When they don't, you'll get an oak tree.'

Caro was suddenly very aware of his arm, slung across the back of the bench behind her. If keeping quiet and still meant they wouldn't disturb the wildlife, then it also meant that she could keep this feeling of being close to Drew for a moment.

A chaffinch flew down onto the path, almost in front of them. A rustle amongst the leaves turned out to be a fox, treading warily and stopping every now and then to sniff the air.

'I never thought that if you stayed still for a moment, you'd see all this.'

Drew smiled. 'We manage these woodlands very carefully to encourage all kinds of different wildlife. We have hedgehog boxes in a more secluded spot over there and if you come down here at night, you can hear them all snuffling around in the undergrowth. There are a few badgers too, and we're thinking about having a beaver enclosure.'

'Beavers? I didn't think you had them in this part of the country.'

'We don't, but they've been reintroduced in enclosures in various parts of England. When they build their homes, a natural wetland forms so you get an increase in those plants and animals too. We're also looking at building a red squirrel enclosure.'

'Don't they catch something from the grey squirrels?' Caro racked her brains for the name of the disease that had decimated red squirrels and came up with nothing.

'Yes, SQPV. Squirrel pox virus. The greys carry the virus, but it doesn't affect them.'

'And that's why you'd have to keep the reds in an enclosure?'

'Yes, there's been some research into administering a vaccine to wild squirrels, but until that's been perfected, it's not possible to establish colonies in England.' He smiled. 'But maybe Mav will take *his* children into these woodlands and find red squirrels roaming free.'

'You're in this for the long haul, then.'

Drew nodded. 'An oak tree can support up to a thousand different species of wildlife. I won't live to see the ones I planted last year grow to their full size.'

'Good thing someone thought to plant a few for us, then.'

'Yes. We're just trying to pay that forward, so that future generations will still have the species that are becoming endangered now. Not just the ones that hit the headlines but the lesser known ones. You know who runs the planet?'

Caro thought for a moment. 'I'm guessing the answer isn't going to be us.'

'Well, in some ways we do. But the wart-biter bush-cricket, the shrill carder bee and the bog sun jumper spider are all endangered species in Britain, and they're part of a vast number of different insects that keep our ecosystem going.'

'Great names. Someone should definitely save them. So saying that I'd rather watch hedgehogs than have a wart-biter cricket crawling across my foot isn't the way to look at it?'

'That's a reasonable enough reaction. But there are a lot of entomologists working very hard to encourage various species of insect, some of which are very important to our natural habitats.' Drew smirked at her. 'It's an endlessly complicated interaction. I thought you might like that.'

It was definitely growing on her. 'I prefer to confine myself to robotics. It's a lot more predictable.'

He nodded, looking up as the sound of voices floated towards them. When Caro saw a young woman, leading a group of children, she automatically moved away from Drew a little, feeling the sweet pressure of his arm around her lift.

'Ah. One of our school trips. They'll be here to see the reindeer.'

'You have reindeer!' Caro couldn't conceal her excitement. '*Real* reindeer?'

'No, they're plastic ones with red noses...' he joked, and Caro frowned at him. 'You want to tag along?'

'Yes. Please. I've never seen a real reindeer before.'

He got to his feet, greeting the woman at the head of the group, and introducing Caro to Angie, a teacher at one of the nearby schools. Drew fell into step with the group, talking to the children and telling them about the wildlife that lived here in the woods.

He was so at ease here. Caro could imagine him tramping these woods, strong and alert to everything that was going on around him. Never alone, because he understood the complex language of the countryside, which Caro had always just hurried past without giving it a second thought. What cacophony did he hear in the rolling waters around her home? Suddenly, she wanted very much to dive with him and find out.

CHAPTER SEVEN

CARO SEEMED AS excited as the children were when they approached the cluster of low barns that housed the petting zoo. Eddie, the manager here, had brought the most docile of the reindeer in from the pasture, and was waiting for them in the barnyard.

A chatter of excitement ran around the group, and Eddie introduced Dasher the reindeer to the children. He saw Caro clutch her hands together, almost jumping up and down with excitement, and Drew decided to hang back a little, sitting down on a bale of hay. The afternoon sun caught the golden highlights in her hair, and he smiled.

Under Eddie's close supervision, each of the children was allowed to approach Dasher, with a little hay to feed him with. Angie took her turn, but Caro was hanging back, talking to a little boy who didn't look inclined to go anywhere near Dasher. They seemed to be coming to some decision, and Caro put her hand up, along with the other kids who wanted to feed Dasher.

She approached Dasher gingerly, turning to look back at the little boy she'd been talking to. Clearly both of them were a little nervous of getting too close to the reindeer. Eddie handed her some straw, and she held it out, seeming ready to snatch her hand away if Dasher made any sudden moves.

Dasher amiably took some of the straw from her hand, and Caro gasped with delight. Carefully, she reached out and stroked Dasher's neck. This was what the petting zoo was for. Kids of all ages.

Meanwhile the little boy was edging closer, emboldened by Caro's bravery. Both Eddie and Caro let him take his time, but finally he reached out, taking some straw to feed to Dasher. Caro turned, and the look of delight on her face made Drew want to laugh out loud with happiness.

'Hey, Drew, I wasn't expecting to see you here this afternoon.' Kirsty, one of the animal care assistants, walked towards him.

'I just dropped in. How's everything going?'

'Fine. Um…are you back at work yet?' Kirsty eyed the walking stick propped up against the bale of hay.

'Yes, I'm back. Anything I can help with?

'Well, I was going to call Ellie but since you're here… I noticed this morning that Missy's very slightly lame in one of her back legs. I've kept her inside, and I think it's just a stone bruise, but it would be great if you could take a look.'

'Yes, of course. You're going to go and help with the children?'

Kirsty nodded. 'Yes, just while Eddie takes Dasher back to the pasture. I'll be as quick as I can.'

'That's okay. I'll wait.'

Drew wondered whether Caro would be going in to see the rabbits with the rest of the group, but when Kirsty ushered them towards the long, low building where the smaller animals were kept, she turned, walking towards him.

'You're not going to see the rest of the animals?'

'No, I've seen a reindeer. That's enough excitement for the day.' Her face was shining, and she plumped herself down on the hay bale next to him. 'The little boy I was with was scared, and I said that I'd go and stroke him for both of us. But he ended up coming to stroke him too, did you see?'

'Yeah, I saw.' The magic of the moment hadn't been lost on Drew. It was so easy to relive the wonder of touching an animal for the first time through her.

'Are we going back to the diving centre? Or do you want to take a rest first?'

'Neither. I've got to take a look at one of the Shetland ponies.' Kirsty had disappeared with the children, and Eddie was leading Dasher back to the pasture, and a thought occurred to Drew. 'I don't suppose you'd come and keep her still for me, would you?'

'I can try. I don't know how to keep a Shetland pony still, though.'

That was one of the things he liked about Caro. She didn't back off from things she knew nothing about, she tried them anyway.

'You just hang onto her bridle. Missy's getting on a bit, and she's not going to give you any trouble.'

He led her into the stable block, found Missy's stall, and showed Caro how and where to hold the bridle. She wrapped her arm around Missy's neck, whispering to her, and Missy quietened. Caro might not have much experience with animals, but she was a natural.

'What's the matter with her?'

'Kirsty thinks she may have trodden on something and bruised the sole of her foot.'

'Ouch! Poor thing. I hate it when that happens.' Caro twisted round, watching as he bent down and lifted Missy's leg a little. 'What are you doing now?'

'Just scraping away the dirt so I can see. It doesn't hurt her.' Drew carefully cleaned the sole with a knife and examined it. There was a red area that looked like a bruise.

'Is she all right?' Caro interrupted his train of thought.

'Hold on. Let me examine her properly.'

Caro gave a little huff of impatience and started whispering to Missy again, who seemed a lot more unconcerned about the procedure than she was. Drew went back to feeling the pulse on Missy's leg and checking the temperature of the sole. He could see no evidence of a cyst or laminitis, which would have been far more serious.

'It looks as if it's just a bruise. She'll need to be rested up a bit, but she'll be fine.'

'Good. D'you hear that, Missy?' Caro was stroking the pony's mane. 'Can I give her something to eat?'

'No, she's fine.' Caro looked so downcast that Drew relented. 'You can give her a little hay from that bale over there.'

Caro scooted out of the stall, pulling at the bale to get a good handful. When Missy took the hay, then nuzzled against Caro's arm, her face lit up again.

It had been so long since he'd really felt the magic he saw in Caro's face. Since he'd felt the wonder she saw in things around her, and in every new experience. Drew could spend a lot of time just watching her and still feel that it wasn't enough.

Kirsty's arrival broke his reverie, and he quickly relayed his findings and went through everything she should do for Missy. Caro gave Missy one last stroke, and then followed him out of the stable.

'Are we going to the diving centre now?' She grinned up at him.

'Wait. Hold on a minute.' Drew shot her a mock-serious look. 'You're taking the afternoon off, even though you haven't worked yourself to a standstill. And you're actually enjoying it?'

Caro's laugh seemed rather more carefree than before. Joyous even. 'Yes, I was wondering about that myself. Seems I am.'

* * *

Kirsty had dropped them off at the diving centre, and Drew found Jake in the office at the back, shuffling through the papers on his desk.

'Drew!' Jake got to his feet and their handshake turned into a hug. 'So you've found us at last.'

'Yeah. I've brought someone to see you.' He turned to Caro, who was hovering in the doorway. 'Caro's interested in scuba diving.'

'Oh, thank goodness for that!' Jake grinned at Caro. 'This paperwork's been driving me crazy.'

Drew chuckled. 'Jake always gets a bit itchy around this time of year. Not so many people want to go diving in the autumn.'

'You can say that again. And I've been missing my diving buddy.' Jake slapped Drew on the back. 'When do you want to go, then?'

'I have to learn first.' Caro gave Jake an apologetic smile.

'Ah. Great. Well, there's an introductory manual I need you to read through...' Jake caught up one of the wire-bound manuals from a large box in the corner of the room, handing it to Caro.

'All of it?' Caro opened the first page, scanning the contents list.

'You can skip chapters six, seven and eleven, they're for the more advanced course.'

'Read all of it.' Drew knew that Jake didn't cut corners, but he wanted Caro to be more than prepared before he took her into the water. Jake shot him a querying look and then shrugged, obviously reckoning that the extra chapters couldn't do her any harm.

'Okay. That's my weekend sorted. Then what?' Caro tucked the manual under her arm.

'Then we do three two-hour sessions in the pool. Now, that'll just give you the basics, and I'd normally suggest you go on a dive with the class after that, but if you're with Drew it'll be fine. He's a qualified instructor.' Jake picked up his diary and flipped through the pages. 'I'm doing lessons next week on Monday, Wednesday and Friday mornings.'

Caro hesitated. Drew knew exactly what she was thinking.

'We could continue with the study on Tuesday and Thursday. I'll be at the clinic on Wednesday, so maybe I could take some of the measurements you need then as well.'

Caro looked at him as if he'd just asked her to cut off her own arm. 'Perhaps it would be better to do the lessons the following week.'

'Then you'll miss out on a few days that week. You can run through everything with me on Tuesday if you like.' Drew already knew exactly what to do, he'd watched Caro do it enough times. But if it made her feel better, she could go through it one more time.

The cogs in her head were working overtime at the moment. Maybe she just didn't trust Drew. Then she turned and smiled at Jake. 'Monday, Wednesday and Friday sounds great, thank you. I'll need to hire a wetsuit as well.'

'Okay, so you have a choice. A thicker wetsuit will probably be all right at this time of year, but a drysuit, like the one that Drew has, will be better.'

'We'll take a drysuit.' Drew interrupted.

'That's going to mean an extra session in the pool, to show you how to deal with the buoyancy and so on. We can do that on Monday afternoon.'

Caro looked a little downcast. Yet more time away from

her work. Then she nodded. 'Okay, in for a penny, in for a pound. I'll hire a drysuit, like Drew says.'

Jake nodded. 'As you're working with Drew, I'll throw the drysuit hire in. We don't have much call for them outside the tourist season.'

'Thank you, but... I don't want to take advantage...' Caro was clearly determined to pay her way.

'Why don't you give Jake a couple of those miniature tortoises? His little boy is two and he'd love them,' Drew interjected.

'Oh, yeah. I heard about those. That's definitely a deal.' Jake grinned. The diving centre was nominally a part of the outreach side of the veterinary clinic, but in practice Ellie and Drew left the management to Jake.

'Four's best. They go crazy, trying to avoid each other, if you put them on a tabletop.' Caro didn't have much concept of bargaining anyone down, but then neither did Jake. The arrangement seemed to suit them both, and Drew decided not to interfere.

'You're coming along to help out, Drew?' Jake was scribbling Caro's name down in his diary.

'Um...no. I said I'd do some work at home on Monday. Friday I'll probably rest up a bit.'

Drew had been so sure that he wanted to show Caro the hidden world that lay beneath the waves, and so sure that she'd be fascinated by it. But now it was turning into a reality, his own fears were kicking in. If he left Caro's training to Jake alone, then there would be no possibility of Drew becoming distracted by her smile or his own fears about taking her into the water and forgetting something vital.

'Okay.' Jake gave him a searching look. He knew that since Luna had died, Drew had given up the responsibility of teaching, and had only gone into the water with experienced divers. But he said nothing.

'Is that all agreed, then?' Drew pushed his fears to the back of his mind. He really needed to get back into the water, and this was a great opportunity. Jake was the best instructor he knew, patient and knowledgeable, and very thorough. Nothing bad was going to happen to Caro. This was an opportunity that no one should miss.

'Yep.' Jake grinned at Caro. 'Monday at nine, then? If you want to come here, I'll give you a lift up to the pool.'

Caro nodded, smiling suddenly. 'Thanks. I'm really looking forward to it.'

Drew had made his mind up not to phone Jake. But Jake knew him too well and phoned him instead, launching exactly into what Drew wanted to hear.

'Has your lady got a photographic memory or something? I got the distinct impression this morning that she had the whole of the manual off by heart.'

'She's not *my* anything. We just work together.' Expressing his relief that Caro had actually read the manual, and absorbed all of the information, might suggest that Drew had entertained the thought that Caro did anything by halves.

Jake chuckled. 'She's a bit too good for you, mate.'

Shorthand for 'Caro would be perfect for you'. Drew had told Jake the very same thing when he'd first set eyes on his wife, and Jake had upped his game significantly in response. Drew had no game left.

'Caro's only interest is her work.' Jake knew what that meant. He'd known Luna.

'Well, she swims like a fish, and she pays attention to every detail. Just thought you might like to know. She's solid, Drew, and she doesn't compromise on safety.'

'Yeah. Thanks.' Drew considered mentioning to Jake that he might like to throw in something unexpected to

gauge Caro's reaction but he was an experienced instructor, and he knew how to test his students.

'I'll catch you later, then…' Drew heard the sound of
Jake's son in the background and knew he had to go.

'Soon. We'll go down to the Hungry Pelican for a pint.'

'Definitely. Tell Caro that Ollie loves the tortoises.
Gotta go…'

The call ended abruptly, and Drew smiled, dropping
his phone on the sofa. Caro would be ready—Jake would
see to that. And his own doubts about going diving again
were receding in the face of wanting to show Caro a part
of the world that he loved. For the first time in a long time
he was beginning to shake off his fears and look forward.

'Want to go for a walk, Phoenix?'

Phoenix twitched her nose. An early evening walk probably didn't sound so fabulously exciting when you were
already curled up in front of the grate. Drew got to his
feet, automatically reaching for his stick and then changing his mind.

'We'll just go a little way. I'll try leaving the stick at
home this time…'

CHAPTER EIGHT

CARO HAD BEEN through her training, and she was ready. Jake had told her she'd be fine. All the same, a little quiver of excited uncertainty had been making her heart pump faster ever since she'd woken up this morning.

She'd carried all her diving equipment down the stone steps and across the beach to her car. Living here *did* have its disadvantages, even if the tides did provide her with the solitude she needed to work. But Drew and Jake didn't see water as any obstacle, and while that was reassuring in someone who was teaching you how to dive, it was rather more challenging when it applied to Drew. More than once she'd woken in the night and wondered what it might be like to look out of her window and see a glimmer of light out to sea as a rowing boat carried him towards her.

Night thoughts. It was the morning now, and Drew was just a friend. If trusting him enough to continue her study alone on Wednesday had been a challenge, then trusting him to take her diving was a piece of cake. There was no need to wonder about the inconsistencies of that, because life could be complicated and inconsistent at times. That was why she liked robots.

She arrived early at the small jetty that was attached to the diving centre and saw Drew walking towards her car to meet her. He was windblown and cheerful, wearing a drysuit with a pair of deck shoes and a windcheater. The stick seemed incongruous next to the spring in his step.

'Hi. Ready to go?'

'As ready as I'll ever be.'

'Got your papers from Jake?'

Jake had bet her another one of the tortoises that Drew would want to see them, and Caro had already paid up. She pulled the list of topics covered and Jake's scores out of her pocket and gave them to him.

Drew scanned them, nodding. 'A hundred percent. Very impressive. Did you bribe Jake?'

He knew full well that she hadn't. 'No, bribery's a contravention of Jake's and my safety standards. Do we change here?'

'Yes, it's easier than trying to do it on the boat.' He led her across to the diving centre and unlocked the main doors. 'The changing rooms are over on the left.'

Locked in the white-painted cubicle, Caro took a deep breath. She was really doing this. She carefully unrolled the drysuit. All she had to do was to apply what she'd learned now. That started with getting into the suit.

First there were layers of clothes to keep her warm, two thermal vests and two pairs of thermal leggings. It took a bit of wriggling and cursing to get into the suit, and she was glad of the zip hook that hung next to the mirror, but she made it. Jake had said that thick socks and trainers would be fine for the boat, and she pulled them on, along with a warm jacket. Bundling her clothes into her bag, she found Drew sitting on the jetty, watching a small blue and white painted fishing boat make its way towards them.

'That's your dad's boat?' It looked a very small craft in which to brave the sea.

'Yep. It looks as if my grandfather's at the helm.'

When the craft neared the jetty, Caro saw a white-haired

man standing alone in the small, white-painted cabin that provided the only shelter from the wind that the boat afforded. He cut the engine and threw a mooring rope to Drew, who caught it expertly and then turned his attention to Caro.

'Welcome aboard, young lady.' He held out his hand in a gesture of old-fashioned courtesy. Caro climbed down the steps from the jetty and found that she was guided onto the deck by a firm, steady grip.

'Thank you, Mr Trevelyan.' The boat wasn't wobbling as much as she thought it might, but it she still had to concentrate on keeping her balance.

'Call me Gramps. No one but the excise man calls me Mr Trevelyan.' Gramps's dark eyes twinkled.

'Leave it out, Gramps.' Drew was handing their diving equipment down to his grandfather and shot Caro a smile. 'He loves to sit in the harbour during the summer and tell all the tourists his smuggling stories. He's never smuggled anything in his life.'

'That's what you know, boy.'

Gramps gave Caro a confiding look, tapping the side of his nose. When he turned his back, Drew rolled his eyes, mouthing his words silently. *'He hasn't.'*

'Where's Dad?' Drew swung down into the boat.

'He's gone off somewhere with your mother.' Gramps shook his head. 'I'll never understand those two if I live to be a hundred.'

Drew shrugged as if he didn't understand either, and Gramps nodded.

'Sit down, lass, we'll be ready to go.' He motioned her towards a bench that ran around the side of the boat and Caro stumbled towards it, sitting down heavily next to the diving gear. Drew sat next to her as the engine of the boat started up again and they began to move across the bay.

'I hope we haven't put your grandfather out. Coming out this morning…' She grimaced awkwardly. Fish out of water was an entirely appropriate cliché as all of this seemed so new and different.

'Nah. The only way you can put Gramps out is to leave him behind on dry land. My parents have a habit of disappearing off together on day trips from time to time.'

'That's nice.' Caro was searching for something to say, and that seemed to be the least contentious, but Drew chuckled.

'My parents are both very different people, and they argued their way through twenty-three years of marriage. Now that they're divorced they get on like a house on fire.'

That seemed very personal information. But in the context of a village, where everyone knew everyone else's business, Caro supposed not.

'I guess…whatever suits them.'

'Yeah. That's my view. They were never going to change each other, although they both tried. Living apart gave them the opportunity to make their peace, and they found that they really liked each other.'

He seemed so at ease out here. As if the wind and the waves were absorbing all the woes that the land held for him. Drew even seemed better on his feet on the rolling deck than he was on land, using handholds on the boat to steady himself instead of his stick. Caro watched the land recede, wondering whether she was going to be sick. A wave of nausea suddenly hit her, and then disappeared as quickly as it had struck.

'You want to take a turn at the helm, lass?' Gramps called back to her, and Drew gave her a nod that indicated this was something of a privilege that wasn't afforded to everyone.

Be brave…

'Yes. Thank you.' Caro eyed the distance between her seat and the helm, wondering how she was going to get there without falling overboard.

'On land you always keep one foot on the ground, yes?' Drew murmured to her, and Caro nodded. 'On a boat, it's one foot on deck, and one hand to hang on with.'

'Right.' Caro got to her feet, grabbing onto the side of the boat. This was easier than it sounded.

Gramps positioned her hands on the helm, pointing to a spot on the horizon. 'Keep your eye right there. That's where we're going.'

Caro nodded. This was easy enough, like steering a car. But the boat seemed determined to go left when she wanted to go right. She turned the wheel a quarter turn, but still couldn't manage to correct their course.

Suddenly she felt a strong body behind her and Drew's hands on hers. 'You need to turn the helm more than you do a steering wheel on a car.' The wheel spun under her fingers, and the boat began to move out of the cove and into the open sea.

'Got it?'

Yes, she had it. But his body felt so warm against her back. So strong. She could so easily just sink into that warmth.

'A bit to the left.' His breath caressed her cheek, and Caro turned the wheel. 'Bit more...'

'You want to go to Trethaven Point? There might be dolphins there.' Gramps's voice reminded her that it wasn't just her and Drew, alone in the universe.

'Dolphins?' She heard the excitement in her own voice and Drew's deep chuckle reverberated through his chest. 'But what about Dolphin Cove?'

'Dolphin Cove got its name from the shape of the headland, which looks like a dolphin's head. If you want to see dolphins, then Trethaven Point's the place to go.'

'Can we go there, then?'

'We'll go wherever you want, lass,' Gramps replied. 'Bear to port.'

'Turn left.' Drew's voice guided her, his hands helping her turn the helm so that the boat described a gentle arc in the water.

It took half an hour to get to Trethaven Point, which was on one side of a huge, sheltered bay. Caro was windblown and very excited, but Drew insisted on checking her dry-suit and all her equipment, turning her round to make sure that everything was just so.

'Now you.' She grinned up at him. 'Jake told us that we must check each other's equipment. He showed us how.'

Drew gave her a lopsided smile. 'Okay. Since Jake told you…'

Caro repeated the acronym that Jake had taught them under her breath, going through the procedure. The boat was bobbing gently at anchor on a calm sea and Gramps was leaning against the helm, his arms folded and with a broad smile on his face as Drew submitted to being turned and turned again as she ran through the checks.

'Happy?' Caro nodded. 'Right, then. Jake's taught you how to sit on the edge of the pool and turn into the water?'

'Yes, he said that was the easiest way for beginners.'

'Okay. I'll go in first and Gramps will help you. Give me the signal when you're ready. You know the hand signal to make if you're in trouble?'

He'd read her papers closely enough, and Jake had given her ten out of ten for hand signals. Caro decided to humour him.

'*Not sure* is this.' She flattened her hand, palm down,

rocking it back and forth. 'And *Help* is this.' She raised her arms above her head.

'Great. Now I want you to stay within reach of me all the time, but if we do get separated, what do you do?'

Caro closed her eyes, visualising the page in the manual and reeled off the bullet points. When she opened them again Gramps was chuckling.

'I think she's good to go, son.'

'All right.' Drew shot Gramps a glare. 'Just making sure…'

Of course he was. Caro had submitted to all of Drew's questions because she knew that he needed to ask rather more that she needed to answer. But she was ready now, and she couldn't wait any longer.

Drew put the regulator into his mouth, holding it in place and executing an impressively smooth back roll into the water. Gramps held out his hand to steady her as Caro swung her legs over the edge of the boat.

'All right, lass?' Gramps smirked. 'Better give him the signal, he'll only make a fuss if you don't.'

Caro signalled an *okay* to Drew and he signalled back. Then a sliding turn brought her into the water with a splash. Now, at last, she could put what she'd learned into practice.

They sank together into a deepening blue, the light dancing on the waves above their heads. The awkwardness of breathing through the regulator and managing the buoyancy of the drysuit were suddenly secondary irritations, compared to the shimmering beauty around her.

Drew was taking this first dive slowly and gently. Keeping within reaching distance and not letting Caro swim as strongly as she knew that she could. But there was enough to fascinate her as they travelled downwards through shoals of small fish to the sea bed. He pointed out crabs and strangely shaped creatures, their large eyes swivelling to take in as much light as possible. Jake had told her about *maerl*, the rock-hard, red skeleton seaweed, and there was some here in the well-lit shallow waters. So many new forms of life that were equipped to deal with their environment. Suddenly tortoise robots seemed just the tip of an ever-expanding iceberg.

It seemed that they'd only been down there for a moment when Drew signalled it was time to surface again. Caro's heart sank, but she knew she must follow his instructions. She'd seen the tension in his face when they'd prepared themselves for the dive.

They surfaced next to the boat, and Caro saw Gramps sitting on the deck, a pair of glasses perched on his nose and reading the newspaper.

'Okay, Gramps?' Drew removed his regulator, shouting up to him.

'Back already?' Gramps raised his eyebrows. 'I haven't got to the sports pages yet.'

Drew grinned. 'You want to go down again, Caro?'

'Yes, please. We haven't seen any dolphins yet.'

He was less solicitous the second time, allowing Caro to dictate the pace a little more. Drew was beginning to enjoy this too, and he even allowed himself to unclip his camera from his belt and take a few photographs. Caro took her time, inspecting the sea floor carefully, and Drew let her to swim a little further.

Finally he tapped his watch, signalling that they should surface again. Caro took one more look at this underwater kingdom, silently bidding it goodbye until the next time. Then she felt Drew's hand on her arm.

He was pointing, towards a flash of movement to their left. It was impossible to see what it was, but then the shapes wheeled around, coming into view. Caro's heart beat a little faster, bubbles spinning upwards from her breathing gear. Dolphins.

She wanted to swim towards them, but Drew had told her she mustn't. She felt his hand curl around hers and she squeezed it tight, watching the creatures whirling playfully in the water. Then they were gone.

He kept hold of her hand. As they drifted back upwards, she wanted to hug him, but was afraid of dislodging some of the breathing gear. When they surfaced, Gramps had abandoned the sports pages and was standing at the side of the boat.

'You saw them, Gramps?' Drew called up to him, and Gramps nodded.

'I managed to catch them on video.' Gramps brandished an up-to-the-minute smartphone, which he presumably kept well hidden when he was playing the old seadog for the tourists.

Caro could have spent all day here, but Drew swam over to the boat, beckoning to her to follow. They climbed aboard, stowing their gear carefully, and then Drew sat down, his face wreathed in a delicious smile.

'You enjoyed yourself?'

'Yes, I did. Thank you so much, Drew. Can we go again?'

He chuckled. 'I think I'm going to insist on it. I've had six months cold turkey, and now I'm well and truly bitten by the diving bug again.'

'Your leg's all right?' Caro had noticed that Drew's movements underwater had been far more effortless than they were on land.

'Yes, no problem. Call it water therapy.'

It had been water therapy in more ways than one. He was smiling and relaxed now. Whether that was because the dive was over, or because he'd finally broken through another barrier in the long climb back to full fitness, Caro wasn't sure. But she was sure that this had been an achievement for Drew and being part of it was special.

He unzipped the pouch at his waist, taking out a smooth flat stone and dropping it into her hand. 'Here. A souvenir of your first dive.'

The stone had a round hole, right through the centre of it. It was the most beautiful thing that Caro had ever seen.

'It's called a *milpreve* in Cornwall. It'll ward off snakes.' Drew glanced at Gramps, who nodded sagely.

'Thank you...' Caro closed her fingers around the stone, holding it to her heart. This morning had been a succession of wonderful things and words weren't enough. And the strangest and most wonderful thing had been that, quite unexpectedly, she'd found herself trusting Drew.

Drew was intoxicated by her eyes. Warm honey brown and reflecting every last bit of the magic of the morning. Caro *was* the magic. The way her forehead had puckered slightly in concentration as she'd quoted the diving manual, which he'd helped Jake to write, straight back at him. The way she'd leaned back a little, almost in his arms, as they'd steered the boat together. The way she'd squeezed his hand under the water.

He watched her as the boat moved steadily back to the diving centre, with Gramps at the helm. Her hair blown dry by the wind and stiff with salt, her fingers a little red from the cold and curled around the cup of hot soup from the flask he'd brought. Her nose was a little red, too, and it was enchanting.

She thanked Gramps, waving to him from the jetty as the boat drew away. Drew opened the diving centre, carrying their tanks inside and leaving them with the others that needed to be refilled. Caro made for the changing rooms, stopping to ask Drew if he'd undo the zip that ran across the back of her shoulders for her. He'd done that a thousand times before for his fellow divers, but it had never seemed so intimate. He decided to wait for her out on the jetty.

She joined him, her face shining. 'Thank you so much, Drew. That was one of the best things I've ever done.'

'Right up there with robotics?' If that was the case, it was praise indeed.

'Definitely. It's given me some ideas as well.' She shot him an impish smile.

'Don't…' Drew held his hands up in an expression of surrender. 'If I find that your tortoise has been banished to a cupboard in favour of a cleaner fish, I'll feel very guilty.'

'That's not going to happen. Tony will always have a place in my heart.'

He should get into his car and go home now. But Caro didn't move, and he couldn't leave. Drew reached out, skimming his fingertips across the arm of her jacket.

'It's been good to get back to diving. Thanks for giving me a good reason.'

She nodded. Caro had a habit of thinking about every aspect of a given situation, and no doubt she'd thought of that, too.

'It must have been hard. After everything that's happened, you must have wondered if it would still be the same.'

'It'll never be the same. But this was as good as the best of what I had before. Better, because…' He shrugged, unable to put his feelings into words.

'Because you knew you'd come close to losing it?'

No. Better because Caro had been there. Something suddenly fell into place and for a moment it seemed as if the void inside him could be filled.

Trapped in her gaze, he reached for Caro's hand, bringing it to his lips. She moved closer, stretching towards him as if she were about to kiss his lips. Then suddenly a tear rolled from her eye and she backed away, her hand over her mouth.

'I'm sorry…' Drew didn't know what he'd done wrong.

'No… It was nice of you. I'm just not that girl…'

She seemed upset. Drew couldn't let this go. 'Not that girl?'

'You know. Pretty girls who say the right thing and don't speak their minds.' Caro wrinkled her nose. Perhaps she thought *that* was speaking her mind a little too plainly.

'You're definitely not that girl, then. You're a beautiful woman who says the things that should be said.' The words came easily because they were true. And suddenly it seemed that Caro needed to hear them.

She blushed suddenly, shaking her head. She really didn't know how beautiful she was, and words weren't enough to convince her. Drew reached for her.

'Caro, I would like very much to kiss you.'

'Would you? Really?' She looked genuinely surprised. 'I'd like to kiss you too.'

He brushed his lips against hers and felt her melt against him. Then he kissed her again, this time a little more insistently. She gasped, smiling up at him, and he kissed her again.

All thought was gone. All he wanted to do was carry her away and make love to her. And then Caro flung her arms around his neck, pulling him down for another kiss that was sweeter and wilder than the rest.

She drew back a little, her eyes still warm with desire. Her hair blowing in the breeze. One last thread of sanity tugged at Drew. They had to stop this.

'This morning… I had the best time. Thank you.' Caro seemed to know that they had to stop, too.

'Yeah. Me, too.' He pressed his lips to her cheek in quite a different kind of kiss. One that allowed the possibility of a parting.

'I think I need to go now.'

'You have work to do?' The thought seemed more bitter to Drew than usual. Caro would always put her work before anything else.

She reached into her pocket, bringing out the stone he'd given her. 'First of all, I have to find somewhere nice to put my *milpreve*. I want to be able to look at it.'

That didn't seem so bad. Caro's rented house didn't contain anything that seemed personal to her, and it was warming to think that this one thing was important enough to her to break that rule.

'I'll let you get on, then.'

If she kissed him again, he wouldn't let her go. Drew stepped back, and all the wild possibilities that had been swirling in his head began to fade.

She nodded, and then turned, shouldering her heavy diving bag, and made for her car. If she looked back...

Caro didn't look back. She already had her eyes set on what was ahead of her, and she'd probably be working late tonight in her workshop to make up for the time she'd lost this week. He watched as she got in and drove away.

That was the first time he'd kissed a woman since Luna had died. Apart from his mother, of course, and Ellie, but that wasn't the same. It was the first time that his body had thrilled to a woman's touch.

And strangely it was all right. Gramps had said that guilt and loss wouldn't always paralyse him, and that one day he'd wake up and find he was moving on. And Luna would have wanted that, her zest for life wouldn't have tolerated him remembering her any other way.

He picked up his stick and began to walk to his car. The

one thing that he couldn't move on from was the present. Caro's work was all-important to her, all-encompassing. That was her choice to make, but Drew had choices too. He couldn't deal with it, and this mustn't happen again.

Why? *Why?* Caro hauled her heavy bag up the stone steps of Smugglers' Top. The morning had been a whole kaleidoscope of delights in all shapes and sizes, the greatest of which had been the Drew-shaped one.

She'd kissed him. It had been wonderful, and Caro was in no doubt that Drew had liked it too. He'd said that she was beautiful, and Drew didn't lie. She'd known he wasn't lying; no one could fake that kind of passion.

And then she'd cut and run, like a scared rabbit.

It was the only thing possible. If she let Drew into her life, then what happened next? The light out at sea? The rowing boat, braving the swell of the tide in the darkness? The knock on her door at midnight by a handsome adventurer? She'd trusted once before, and then she'd lost one of her most important projects *and* her home.

She balanced the equation carefully in her head. On one side, Drew. On the other side, everything else. If he seemed to outweigh everything else, then that was just faulty calculation.

She dumped her bags in the hall and walked into the bathroom, staring at herself in the mirror. Her fingers grazed her lips, and she could almost feel his kiss, still there.

Beautiful. The word made her smile.

'Nonsense,' she reproved her reflection. Drew had reclaimed a part of his life this morning, and it was natural that he would feel a sense of euphoria. He'd got carried away.

She took the *milpreve* from her pocket, turning it over

in her hand. It *had* been a wonderful morning, and the glistening stone, worn smooth by the sea, would always remind her of his kiss. But now she had work to do.

CHAPTER NINE

CARO WAS BRIGHT and early on Monday morning, and looking as smart as she always did when she visited the clinic. The briskness of her manner told Drew that she'd made the same resolution as he had. Their kiss had been wonderful, and if it had settled the question about whether Caro was beautiful or not, he would be completely happy. But it was something that shouldn't be repeated.

'I made something. It's a thank-you gift for the clinic.' She dumped the box she was carrying in front of him on his desk.

'That's nice. May I open it?'

'If you don't, it's not going to be a great deal of use, is it.'

Okay. Logic trounced pretty much everything else in Caro's book. Drew flipped open the lid of the box and saw a small robot dog crouched at the bottom.

'Oh. That's great. Thank you.' Drew wasn't quite sure what they were going to do with it, they had enough *real* dogs around here, but it was a nice thought.

'You haven't seen what it does yet.'

He lifted the dog out of the box and tried to stand it on its legs on his desk. The legs weren't stiff enough to hold the body and the dog collapsed into a sitting position. Maybe there was something wrong with it.

'It's supposed to be lying down. This is a very specific, sole-purpose dog.'

Sole-purpose dogs were a new one on Drew, but he went with the flow. No doubt Caro was about to dazzle him with something clever. 'What's its sole purpose?'

She rolled her eyes as if that should be obvious to him. 'I noticed last week that there was a pup in an incubator. It seemed a bit lonely.'

The pup had been very sick, although it was improving now. It had had blankets and a favourite toy but hadn't taken much notice of either. Drew found the on switch for the robot, hidden behind its ear, and pressed it. The robot's small frame began to expand and contract in a regular rhythm.

'It's breathing!'

Caro gave him a reproving look, but obviously decided that she didn't need to tell him that it wasn't *actually* breathing, just that its chest was moving up and down.

'I've heard about breathing pet comforters, and it seemed like a good idea. If the pup's mother were with it, she'd be breathing.' Caro frowned. 'She'd be furry, too.'

'Well…yes.' There was that to it, but breathing was a good start. 'I guess we could make it a coat.' He wondered how Caro might feel about the clinic making alterations to her designs.

Finally, she smiled. 'Yes, that's what I was hoping you might do. You know best the kind of thing that would be most comforting and what's hypo-allergenic and so on. I'd like you to complete the design.'

Drew was conscious of the honour that was being accorded them. Caro never hesitated in asking for the information she needed. But she didn't just turn her half-finished designs over to someone else for the finishing touches.

'Thank you. This is really amazing. Perhaps we can get Tegan to sew it a furry coat while she's sitting at the reception desk.' Perhaps not. On second thoughts, Tegan probably didn't do a lot of sewing but Drew didn't rule out the possibility that she might have hidden talents in that direction. He decided that the question of who would actually do the sewing could be shelved for the moment.

'So you like it?'

'It's a brilliant idea Caro, thank you. You did this at the weekend?' Drew wondered whether she'd had any sleep at all.

'It didn't take long. I've got templates for all kinds of dogs that do all kinds of things. The thing that took longest was printing out the body, and I just set the printer going and went to bed.'

That was a relief. 'I'm going to show Ellie and Lucas.' He picked up the dog, switched it off again, and made for the door. 'Are you coming?'

It seemed that the appeal of the dog had ended now that he'd confirmed that it was fit for purpose, and the problem at hand had been solved. 'You go. I'll go and calibrate the equipment in your surgery, if that's okay.'

'Sure. Go ahead. And thanks again, Caro, this is an innovative solution.'

That made her smile. Caro was all about solutions. Drew tucked the dog under his arm, surreptitiously switching it back on again as he walked along the corridor. Caro had got the movement just right, and it really did feel as if it were breathing. Unless he was very much mistaken, Ellie would love this.

Back to normal. It was a relief, even if it was a disappointment as well. Drew hadn't mentioned the kiss once. Caro had thought that was an excellent idea and neither had she.

Ellie had made a great fuss over the breathing dog, although its movements and reactions were so simple as to be verging on the mundane. Drew seemed to want everyone to like the robot, and Caro was secretly pleased at the pride with which he showed it around.

Caro had agreed to make another two of the dogs, and Ellie had insisted that the clinic should pay for them. When Caro had refused any payment, Drew had stepped in and settled the matter by ordering a box of printer filaments in return for the dogs.

He'd promised to help put the dogs together, and Caro had left the larger plastic pieces to print overnight. But almost as soon as he arrived at Smugglers' Top the following morning, his phone rang. He listened carefully to the voice at the other end of the line, his face darkening.

'I'm sorry. I have to go.'

'You've only just got here.' It wasn't like Drew to allow anything to interrupt what he was doing, and this must be important. 'What's the matter?'

'That was Ellie. There's been an oil spill out at sea...' He shook his head, running his fingers through his hair.

'Is it bad?'

'We don't know the scope of it. Just that an oil tanker's run into trouble, and the crew have been airlifted off. Apparently it's still afloat, and it's being towed, but there is an oil slick forming.'

He looked worried. Ashen.

'What are you going to do?'

'Ellie says that there's help on the way from the environmental agencies, but they won't arrive until later in the day. We're here now.' He'd already pulled his jacket on and was halfway to the door. Phoenix seemed to sense the urgency in his movements and was trotting quietly behind him.

'Wait. Drew, I'll come with you.'

He turned, his hand on the door latch. 'It's not your battle, Caro.'

'What, because I'm not from Cornwall? We've only got one sea, and it's as much mine as it is yours. Don't you dare tell me it's not my battle.'

'It's going to be hard work. Distressing at times, too.'

'Well, if you're up to it, I'm sure I am.'

Drew smiled suddenly. 'Okay. Bring a warm sweater and your drysuit. We can lend you an oilskin jacket.'

Luckily, the drysuit that she'd been lent was packed neatly away in her diving bag, along with the warm underclothes that she wore with it. Caro pulled on a thick sweater, following him down the stone steps and onto the beach. They bundled into his car, and Drew stopped off outside a stone cottage in the village, going inside for a moment and then reappearing with his own diving gear. When they reached the harbour, it seemed full of people who knew exactly where they were going and what they were doing, loading boats and setting out to sea.

She saw Lucas and Ellie exchanging a kiss before they split up to board separate boats. Jake wound his way through the crowd, catching up with them.

'Can I hitch a lift?'

Drew nodded. 'Of course. I need to speak to Lucas before we go. I'll catch up with you at the boat.'

Caro could see Drew's father's boat further along the quay. A woman, with shoulder-length blonde curls, dressed in a woollen coat that incorporated all of the colours of the rainbow, was hurrying towards it, carrying two large bags. The man on board, who looked too much like Drew not to be his father, stopped to greet her.

Jake nudged her. 'That's Diana, Drew's mother. She never lets Peter go to sea without sandwiches and a flask.'

The bag that Diana handed to Peter looked as if it contained a lot of sandwiches and more than one flask. Caro watched as Drew's parents hugged, Diana's long scarf fluttering in the breeze.

Diana bade Peter goodbye and then turned away, catching sight of Caro.

'Ah! You must be Caro.' She thrust the second bag into Caro's arms. 'Drew texted me and asked me to bring my oilskin jacket for you. Here.'

'Thank you. I'll look after it and make sure I get it back to you.' Caro put the bag at her feet, holding out her hand to Diana, who shook it vigorously.

'I've been telling Peter that he must make sure that Drew doesn't hurt his leg again.' Diana leaned confidingly towards Caro and Jake. 'Of course he's a Trevelyan, so he doesn't listen. They all think that they have everything under control and no one needs to worry about them. They'll never change.'

'I'll keep an eye on him,' Jake volunteered.

'Would you, darling? Thank you.' Diana turned to Caro. 'I've been hearing all about you. You're up at Smugglers' Top, inventing marvellous things…' Diana gave a wave of her hand to cover the full range of marvellous things.

'I'm doing my best.' Caro smiled, warming immediately to Diana.

'Fabulous. Creativity's such an important thing. And Jake's been giving you diving lessons…?'

'Try not to make it sound as you've been stalking her, Mum.' Drew's voice sounded behind her. 'Caro's not used to village gossip, she's still under the impression that not everything she does is common knowledge within ten minutes.'

Diana waved her son away. 'Don't listen to him. I'd be fascinated to hear more about your inventions, we must have tea together. There's a little place overlooking the harbour that does a very passable afternoon tea.'

'Thank you. I'd like that.'

'Wonderful.' Diana smiled at her, and then turned to her son. 'Drew, darling, you *will* be careful, won't you? I know that there's no point in asking you to stay behind, but I just couldn't bear it if you were hurt again…'

Drew wrapped his arm around his mother's shoulders, taking her to one side and speaking to her quietly. They must have been words of reassurance because Diana was nodding, and when Drew let her go, she seemed reconciled to his leaving.

Gramps came hurrying along the quay and got into the boat. Drew and Jake followed him, and Drew turned to help Caro. Peter gave Diana a cheery wave, and she waved back, her bright scarf fluttering in the sunshine as they drew away from the dock.

Drew and Jake were talking to Peter, who was at the helm. Gramps patted the wooden bench beside him in an invitation to join him.

'All right, lass?'

'I think so. This is all very sudden, and everyone seems so concerned.'

Gramps nodded. 'Oil spills have done a lot of damage along this coastline. Drew doesn't remember the worst of them, but he's seen the effect it had on marine life. It strikes a cold feeling in the heart.'

'Maybe it's not so bad. Drew said they don't know yet.'

'That's right, lass. We all need to hope for the best.'

The boat lurched, and Caro felt suddenly sick. She clapped her hand over her mouth.

'Bit queasy?' Gramps leaned towards her.

'When I came out last time, I felt a bit sick for a while. Then it passed off again.'

'Come and stand by the helm. You'll feel better there.'

Whatever worked. A cold sweat was beginning to form on the back of her neck and Caro was glad of Diana's thick oilskin jacket.

'Out of the way, lads.' Gramps selected the spot where Caro should stand and pointed to it.

Drew turned to her. 'Feeling sick? Take a few deep breaths. And don't look down at the deck, look at the other boats. If your brain can gauge the movement, then your stomach will feel better.'

'Or you could just give her a ginger biscuit.' Peter glanced around at her. 'I dare say Diana's packed a few, she usually does.'

'Yeah. That's a good one too.' Drew reached over to the bag that Diana had packed, unzipping it and bringing out a box of home-made biscuits. 'There you go. Mum never forgets.'

Caro nibbled at the biscuit, chewing on the small chunks of ginger. It was difficult to say which of the remedies had worked but she was feeling better now and ready to take on the task in hand. Up ahead, there was an oleaginous sheen across the water, and as they came closer, Caro could see that the white specks that dotted the surface were sea birds.

Drew's face became grim again. Caro moved out of the way as Gramps took the helm and Peter started to talk on the radio. He turned to Drew.

'Ellie says it's a smallish patch of oil, they've just been all the way around the edge of it. Most of the birds are in this quadrant.'

Drew nodded. 'So we'll start here?'

'Yes. Her boat will be joining us shortly, and Lucas is staying over the other side.'

The boat was going slower now and Caro could see a

bird in the sea alongside it, smeared with oil and struggling vainly to fly.

'Drew...!' She tugged at his sleeve and his gaze followed the line of her pointing finger. 'Can we get it?'

'That's what we're here for.' Drew opened the storage compartment, under the bench at the back of the boat, taking out two long-handled nets and a bundle of flat-packed cardboard boxes. Pulling a box into shape, he set it down on the deck then picked up one of the nets, trailing it in the water next to the bird. It flapped and squawked, but it was too weak to put up much resistance, and Drew netted it and swung it back onto the deck.

'Are we going to take the oil off now?' Caro couldn't bear to see the poor creature in such distress.

'No, we can't. Cleaning oil off a bird is a traumatic process, and they're already exhausted. We'll keep them at the clinic for at least a day, feed them and keep them warm until they regain their strength.' Drew carefully extricated the bird from the net, laying it down in the box.

'Okay. So we're just collecting them.'

'Yes, both live birds and dead ones. We need to remove as many of the carcasses from the sea as we can to prevent secondary poisoning of predators.'

'What do you want me to do?'

Drew handed her the net. 'Take this and net as many as you can reach. Bring them back to me and I'll put them into the boxes. If you can't reach, don't lean over the side. The most important thing is that you don't fall overboard.'

'Gotcha. Most importantly, don't fall in.'

Suddenly the task ahead of her seemed impossible. Trying to rescue half-dead birds from a polluted sea. It already made her want to cry, and she looked down at the deck, embarrassed at her own faint-heartedness.

'Hey.' She felt his finger curl under her chin, and when

she raised her gaze his face was tender. 'I'm really glad you're here, Caro. I would have left you back at home, but you wanted to do something, and you came with me. That means a lot.'

He wanted her here. Maybe even needed her, just a little. Bravery flooded back into her heart. Clutching the net, Caro walked over to the side of the boat.

It was hard work, both physically and emotionally. For as many birds that she leaned over and pulled alive from the sea, there were many more that were dead. Drew examined each bird that she and Jake netted, putting the dead ones into a large box with as much care as he took with the live ones. He fed the weakest birds with a gastric tube, keeping them warm by wrapping them in old towels. He was tireless, and every time Caro wanted to give up, she knew that she only had to look at Drew to receive a smile.

Gramps was manoeuvring the boat slowly and skilfully through the water, while Drew's father was using binoculars to spot the birds. After three hours of back-breaking work, Drew decided that they should take the birds they'd rescued back to the clinic.

Suddenly Caro was very hungry. Very tired. She stripped off her gloves, sitting down next to Drew at the stern of the boat, and he reached into Diana's bag, taking out one of the flasks and pouring some hot chocolate for her. As the boat swung round, he reached out to steady her, keeping his arm firmly around her shoulders as Gramps piloted the boat away from the oil.

CHAPTER TEN

THE BOATS CARRYING Ellie and Lucas were also making their way across the bay, and there were people waiting to receive the boxes of birds. Ellie jumped onto the dock, supervising their transfer up to the clinic, and Lucas was carefully unloading the boxes from the boats. Even Tegan was there, wearing a pair of pink wellingtons and a spotted pink mac, with heavy gloves to protect her nails.

They waited until the other boats had left the dock to make space for them, and then Gramps manoeuvred alongside it. Tegan was coaxing him off the boat with the promise of a cup of tea, and Ellie took his arm, leading him up to the clinic. He was obviously tired, and it seemed he wasn't going to be allowed back out on the boats this afternoon.

Dry land seemed a little strange now, and when Caro got back onto the boat, the movement of the deck seemed far more normal. Ellie was staying behind to supervise the care of the birds, and she stood on the beach, waving at the boat carrying Lucas away from her.

'Goodbye, my lover...' Her accent had taken on a broad Cornish twang. *My lover* was an endearment used for practically anyone, but it was clear that Ellie only had one lover and that it was Lucas.

'Looking at them together now, it's hard to believe that they spent six years apart,' Drew reflected.

Now they were happy, calling out for everyone to hear. And Drew said that people could never change.

'They've changed…' She ventured the hypothesis.

He turned suddenly, raising one eyebrow. 'Nah. Lucas and Ellie were always made for each other. Nothing ever changed, things are just back the way they were always meant to be.'

Jake beckoned to him and Caro was left alone, staring out to sea. A movement over to their left caught her eye. Drew was talking to Jake, and Peter had his eyes on the waves in front of them, so no one else had noticed. Caro hurried to fetch the binoculars, training them as best she could on a moving target.

A sick feeling rose in her stomach as the deck lurched unexpectedly beneath her feet. But she'd seen all she needed to see.

'Drew! There's some wreckage over there. And something's moving.'

Drew hurried across to her, taking the binoculars and training them on the horizon. He turned to Peter. 'Dad, there's something there. Maybe a small dolphin or a seal. The water's clear around it, but it's caught in some wreckage.'

Peter nodded, swinging the helm, and they changed course. As they got closer, Caro could see that it *was* a dolphin, and that the sea around it contained a larger shape, which was circling the creature.

'It's a baby…and the mother's there.' Drew pulled the radio speaker from its clip, speaking into it, and Caro saw Lucas's boat turn towards them.

'What are we going to do? Can we get it on board?'

Drew shook his head. 'If the baby's not badly injured, superficial cuts will heal in the sea. We don't want to take the baby away from its mother if we can help it, not least because there's the risk that the mother might attack us.'

'But...dolphins are friendly, aren't they?'

'They're wild animals. And her instinct is to protect her young.' Drew's face was set in concentration. 'Are you up for coming in with us?'

'Yes, of course.' Drew wouldn't have asked if they hadn't needed her help.

'Great.' He nodded at Jake, who disappeared down the tiny hatch that led below deck. 'You take the cabin; we'll need our drysuits.'

Jake reappeared, hauling the men's diving bags with him. Peter helped her down the steps, and Caro found herself in a tiny cabin, two bunk beds on one side and a row of cupboards on the other. There was about two feet of clear space between the two and everything was rolling from side to side, the movement making Caro feel a little queasy again.

At least there wasn't far to fall. And she'd been given the luxury of a cabin to change in while Drew and Jake changed on deck.

Caro took off her sweater and jeans, putting on the thick vests and leggings that went under the drysuit. Then she crawled into the bunk, unpacking her drysuit. She could just about manage to roll it down and get her feet into it...

A tap sounded at the door. 'Are you decent?'

More or less. The sound of Drew's voice made her feel virtually naked. And the thought of him squeezing with her into this tiny space brought a hot flush to her cheeks. But she wasn't used to this, and she was going to need some help.

She leaned over, opening the cabin door. When Drew entered, the available space seemed to dwindle to nothing.

He was wearing just a thermal singlet and thick sweat-pants, and his shoulders looked very broad.

'These things are a bit tricky until you get used to them.' His voice sounded much the same as it did when he was talking to one of the dog owners at the clinic. Very professional.

She could do this. Caro fixed her thoughts on the baby dolphin, which needed their help. Drew set about helping her to get her feet into the drysuit and pulling it up over her legs.

'Okay, stand.'

Standing involved allowing him to wrap his arms around her to lever her out of the bunk. They were squeezed face to face now and Caro focussed her eyes on his chest, wishing that she could manage to think about something other than the warmth of his skin.

'Put your arms in.' Some wriggling and tugging ensued, and then Drew pulled the headpiece over her head, leaning round to do up the zip that ran across the back of her shoulders.

'Comfortable?'

The drysuit was fine. She was about to explode...

'Yes, I'm good. Thanks.' She made the mistake of looking up at him. The quickly hidden mischief in his eyes told her that she wasn't the only one who had been considering the possibilities of their being squished together in a restricted space.

'My pleasure.' He backed away, leaving her to take a shaky breath and follow him back up on deck.

Jake was already in the water, along with Lucas and one of the men from his boat. Drew was stepping into his drysuit with the ease that years of practice afforded.

'Here's what we'll do.' Drew was using his *listen carefully* tone and Caro focussed her gaze on his face, trying not to think about the strong, capable hands that had eased her into her suit.

'Jake, Lucas and Terry will be taking the mother and holding her in the water next to her baby, which should calm them both. It looks as if the baby's tangled in some plastic mesh, and if you help me hold it, I should be able to cut it free. You must try to keep its blow hole above the surface or it'll drown.'

'I can do that.'

He nodded, giving her a smile. Pride began to warm Caro's heart. Drew was relying on her and she wouldn't let him down.

'There are a few spots of oil in the water around the wreckage. Try not to swallow any or get it on your skin. Wear your goggles, they'll protect you.' She felt Drew's fingers curl around hers, and he gave her hand a squeeze. Then he was all business again, pulling the headpiece of his suit into place.

Peter handed him a diving bag, while Caro pulled on her flippers. Their exchanged *okay* signal seemed to carry with it more warmth than just a normal safety procedure, and she eased herself into the water, swimming with Drew towards the wreckage.

Lucas, Jake and Terry had managed to manoeuvre the mother dolphin alongside her baby, which was emitting high-pitched whistles, trying to get free from the plastic mesh in which it was caught and only getting more entangled. Treading water, Drew tried to soothe the frightened creature, and it reacted to his presence.

When Caro wrapped her arms around the baby dolphin it was warm to the touch. She stroked its head and it seemed to calm a little. She glanced at Drew and he smiled.

'That's right. You're doing fine.'

The other three men were having a bit more trouble. The

mother was large and strong, and they struggled to keep hold of her, but she was calmer now that she was with her baby. Drew was between the two of them, tending to the baby, but they could see and hear each other, and seemed to be communicating, making sharp trilling noises.

Drew cut the mesh with a knife, looking carefully for any signs of injury as he went. The mother lashed her tail, bumping against his back a few times, but Jake and Lucas were holding her steady, keeping her quiet. Caro wondered if she knew that they were there to help.

Everyone was cool and calm, watching the dolphins carefully while he worked. It took half an hour to cut the little dolphin free, and then Drew wiped the specks of oil from around its blow hole. Caro's arms were aching and she was beginning to tire, but it only took one look at Drew to shore up her resolve.

He signalled to her to get her attention. 'Keep hold of the baby. I need to clear some of this wreckage away before we release them.'

Caro held the little dolphin as tightly as she dared while Drew pushed the wreckage out from under it. Finally, Drew seemed satisfied that the dolphin was unhurt, and they could release it. He ducked under the baby, surfacing next to Caro and helping her to hold the small creature.

'We'll release them on my count...' He looked around, receiving the okay signal from the others. 'Three... Two... One.'

Everyone let go. The baby shot forward, its wake pulling her forward in the water. As the mother followed, Caro felt a heavy blow on her chest that drove the air from her lungs and spun her backwards. Instinctively she closed her eyes and held her breath as she felt herself hit the water and her head went under.

She was drifting. Dazed. Before she could wrap her

head around what had happened, she felt someone next to her and when she opened her eyes, she saw that it was Drew. His arm snaked around her waist and then their heads broke the surface together.

She heaved in a breath, choking and clinging to him. Okay. She was okay. Shakily she gave the sign, still gasping for air, and feeling her shoulder twinge as she raised her arm.

There was no need to do anything more. Drew supported her back to the boat and together he and Jake boosted her up onto the deck.

'I'm all right...' Jake sat her down and took her goggles off. Then Drew elbowed him away. Apparently this was *his* job.

He leaned her forward, making sure that she could breathe properly. 'Did you swallow any water?'

'No... I don't think so.'

'Okay. Where were you hit?'

'On the side of my chest. My shoulder hurts a bit. What happened?'

'The mother caught you with her tail as she swam away. She lifted you right out of the water.'

'Uh...' Caro put her hand to her shoulder, flexing it. It didn't feel too bad... 'Are they okay?'

'Yeah, they're fine.' Jake had been watching the progress of the pair, and he indicated their curved wake. They seemed to be circling the boats, keeping their distance in case anyone decided to try to capture them again.

'Good. That's good.'

Drew had stripped his drysuit down to his waist, and she felt the brush of his skin against her cheek as he reached around to undo the zip that ran across the back of her shoulders. Actually, she *was* feeling a little shaky. She could do with a hug right now, but she didn't dare ask.

Drew carefully eased the headpiece over her head, rolling the drysuit down. As he did so, Peter wrapped a blanket around her shoulders.

'I'm okay.'

'So you said. Take a deep breath for me.' Drew's voice was gentle, and she felt his fingers on her ribs, feeling for any injury. Her ribs felt fine. His hands…a lot better.

She let him gently test her arms and shoulders, feeling warmth flow through her. It was probably about time she called a halt to this; she was enjoying it far too much.

'Any headache or stiffness in your neck? Do you feel sick?'

'I've no symptoms of a concussion. It's just my shoulder, Drew. And I can move it okay, I think it's just bruised.'

He nodded, wrapping the blanket around her. His eyes were gentle but his mouth formed a tense line.

'I'm so sorry, Caro…' He turned to Peter. 'Dad, we should go back.'

'No! I don't want to go back.' Caro frowned at him. 'And it's not your fault, she could have hit any one of us. I *told* you that I wanted to come and help.'

'The lady has a point.' Jake was leaning against the side of the helm, his arms folded. He held up his hand in a gesture of surrender when Drew turned and glared at him.

Peter stepped in to settle the matter. 'Let's get you down into the cabin, Caro, and out of that suit. Drew, you can bring some hot chocolate. Jake, take the helm for me.'

'Aye-aye, Cap'n.' Jake grinned. Drew hesitated and then nodded, helping Caro to her feet and allowing his father to guide her down into the cabin.

Drew stripped off his drysuit, putting on jeans and deck shoes, and then grabbed the flask of hot chocolate. His father appeared from the cabin, bringing Caro's dripping drysuit with him and signalling to him that he could go down to see her now.

He should get a grip. Caro was all right, but she'd had a shock and she needed him to be calm. She was sitting on the bunk, the blanket wrapped around her shoulders and legs, a small puddle still on the floor where his father had helped her out of the drysuit.

'I won't fuss.' He poured the hot chocolate and handed it to her.

'That's okay. You can fuss a bit.' She gave him an intoxicating smile. 'And I reckon you've still got your training wheels on.'

As usual, she'd managed to divine exactly what he was thinking. Luna's death and his own injuries had made him acutely aware of the senseless accidents that could happen and their consequences. He'd do anything…anything…to stop Caro from being hurt.

'I guess I have. Thanks for putting up with me.'

'No problem.' She took a sip from her cup. 'Take a look, will you?'

She let the blanket fall from her shoulders, handing him the cup. Caro eased herself carefully out of her long-sleeved thermal top, and he saw she had a sleeveless vest on underneath. He was both grateful and disappointed that she'd taken Jake's usual advice about layers of clothing, but on reflection he should probably go with grateful.

He was becoming aware that his leg was aching, so he sat down on the bunk next to her. Drew inspected her shoulder carefully, flexing her arm again, and her face showed no pain. A red mark showed where a bruise was beginning to form and she tried to squint down at it.

'How does it look?'

'Not so bad. You'll have a bruise.'

'I'm glad you were there, Drew. Thank you.'

'It's what diving buddies are for.' Caro was a lot more than just a diving buddy to him, but he couldn't go the whole hog in emulating her habit of saying exactly what was on her mind.

'And I could do with a hug.'

'So could I.' Drew curled his arms around her. She nestled against his chest and he felt the last of his own shakiness subside.

Haltingly, she began to whisper. The shock of the blow. Feeling afraid but knowing she was safe when he'd caught hold of her. All of the things that Drew had never talked about when he'd had his accident, and which he probably should have. She voiced her fears and then put them aside, snuggling against him as if he was her comfort.

Maybe a little closer. Maybe a little longer, although Peter and Jake might start wondering what they were doing. He dared to plant a kiss on the top of her head, and then he let her go.

'You'll give the nets a rest for a while?' This time his question didn't involve any of the push and pull between concern and wanting to be strong.

'Yes, I think I will.' She gave him an impish look. 'I suppose that means we're staying out here for a bit longer?'

Drew sighed. 'Yes. We're staying.'

Caro grinned at him as he walked out of the cabin, and Drew took the stairs with renewed energy, using the rails to boost himself upwards. They had work to do.

CHAPTER ELEVEN

THEY DIDN'T MANAGE to collect as many seabirds as they had this morning, but that was largely because there were fewer stuck in the oil. Most of the ones they did find alive were in bad shape, and there were a few other marine creatures as well, a dead starfish and an octopus. They heard over the radio that the boat Lucas was working from had rescued a sea otter and was heading back to the clinic.

They were all tired, and the sun was sinking low on the horizon. Peter turned the boat and they made for home. Drew looked over his shoulder more than once, obviously thinking the same as Caro. The job was only half-finished, and there was still more to do, but they'd done all they could today.

Ellie and Lucas were at the dock and helped to unload the boxes of birds. Caro saw Jake stride across to a woman who was carrying a drowsy two-year-old, hugging them both and kissing his son before they walked to their car together. Drew asked Lucas if there was anything he could do at the clinic and was told no.

'The tide will be in soon.' Drew walked to his car with Caro in the gathering dusk.

'Yeah, I'd better be getting back.'

'Or you could come to the Hungry Pelican and we'll get

something to eat. You can stay at mine tonight, and we'll be ready to go back out again in the morning.'

No question about whether she was going or not. He knew that he couldn't keep her away.

'I've heard the food's really good there, Ellie's mum and dad run it?'

Drew chuckled. 'That's right. You must be getting used to village life if you're hearing gossip. Although as it goes, that isn't all that juicy.'

'I might have to try and do something with my hair first…'

'Your hair's fine. No one dresses up for the Hungry Pelican.'

The quayside pub was already busy, and Caro excused herself to go to the rest room while Drew made his way to the bar. She combed her hair, wincing as her shoulder protested and the comb snagged in a knot. At least the day at sea had brought a bit of a glow to her cheeks, and that, along with fixing her hair back in a slightly lopsided plait, was about as good as it was going to get.

Drew was talking to a man behind the bar, who had a shock of white hair. He introduced him as Gordo Stone, and the man leaned over to shake her hand.

'I'm Ellie's dad. I heard you've been out with Drew today.'

'Yes, we just got back.'

'Ellie says it's not as bad as we'd feared.'

Drew shook his head. 'It's a small spill. Hopefully it won't be coming onto the shore.'

Gordo nodded. 'What are you having?'

'I'll have a sparkling water.' Drew turned to her. 'Do you want to try the local brew?'

Gordo was already moving towards the pump and there seemed to be no escaping it. 'I'll have a half, thank you.'

Drew reached for his wallet and Gordo shook his head. 'First round's on me for everyone who's been out today. Something to eat, Caro? We do a mean fish and chips, even if I do say so myself.'

'Fish and chips sounds great. A large portion, please.'

Drew chuckled. 'Gordo doesn't know how to do small portions. Same for me too, please.'

'Right you are.' Gordo turned, shouting to someone who was working in the kitchen behind the bar, and then got their drinks for them.

Both Gordo and Drew were looking at her, and it appeared that she was expected to taste hers now. She took a sip.

'Mmm. This is *very* good.'

Gordo nodded in approbation and turned to his next customer, while Drew guided Caro over to a table by the fire. When their food arrived, the chips were good as well. And the fish was delicious. They were both hungry.

'Oh.' Caro leaned back in her seat, surveying her empty plate. 'That was lovely.'

Drew was looking pleasantly relaxed now too. He seemed to know everyone here, exchanging a few words with whoever happened to walk past their table.

'You want another drink?'

'What I'd really like is a hot shower and a bed.' Caro wondered whether she should emphasise that both would be alone as she saw that flash of mischief in his eyes again. No, alone went without saying.

'Me too.' He got to his feet, making his way over to the bar, and Caro grabbed her coat and followed him.

'You can put that away.' Gordo had seen Drew's wallet in his hand.

'What's the matter, Gordo? Won the lottery?' Drew raised his eyebrows.

'I'll take your money next time you're in here.' Gordo propped his elbow on the beer pumps. 'But no one would have expected you to go out today, Drew. Not so soon after the accident.'

'You'll take something from me?' Caro had been feeling for her purse at the bottom of her bag and finally found it.

Gordo laughed. 'My Ellie doesn't know when she's beaten either. Off with you both, before I throw you out.'

Drew chuckled, leaning over the bar to shake Gordo's hand. Then he ushered Caro through the door and into his car.

'That was nice of him.' Ellie settled into her seat as Drew drove through the narrow lanes to his cottage.

'He and Wyn are great. I used to hang out with Ellie at their place quite a bit when we were kids and my mum and dad were arguing.'

'You and Ellie…you never thought about getting together?'

Drew let out an explosive laugh. 'What? No. Ellie and I practically grew up together, she's the sister I never had. I think there were about ten minutes, when we were sixteen, when I realised that she might be pretty.'

Caro raised her eyebrows. 'What? Ellie's gorgeous.'

He shrugged. 'She's my friend. I tend not to notice things like that about her.'

But he'd said that he found Caro beautiful. It was better not to think about that, particularly if she was spending the night at Drew's place.

'It must be nice. To have a friend like that.'

'Yeah, it is.' He stopped the car outside his cottage. 'You don't?'

'No. Like I said, my parents moved around a lot, they still do. It's tough enough to keep up with them, let alone anyone else.'

'Apart from the robots.'

Suddenly that didn't seem enough. If she'd had some-where like this to call home... Caro could see why Drew never wanted to leave.

'I noticed something at the pub tonight.' It was time for a change of subject.

'Yeah?'

'All of the people who stopped to talk to you... Not one asked you how you were.'

He thought for a moment. 'No, I don't believe they did. Perhaps telling everyone exactly the same thing is start-ing to work.'

'Or perhaps it's just that you seem so much better. You're hardly using your stick now and you move much more confidently.'

'My leg still hurts from time to time, but I don't feel as if it's going to give way under me.' He shrugged. 'My physio told me that I'd get to the point where suddenly I started to forget all about it.'

He broke off suddenly, gazing at her. Nothing that was ever said or done between them made Caro shiver quite so deliciously as the silences. And this silence told her that she'd helped him forget that he was a recovering invalid and remember who he really was.

Drew had done that all by himself. She might have been there when he finally made that transition, but Caro couldn't take any of the credit for it. All the same, the warmth of his gaze was compelling, and for a moment she couldn't break free.

Finally, Drew moved. 'Let's get inside.'

His cottage was...just Drew all over. She could imag-ine him on winter evenings in the book-lined sitting room, sprawled on the comfortable sofa. Surrounded by the things he loved, stones and shells on the mantelpiece and in front of the rows of books memories dredged up from the sea. Photographs on the wall, of boats, divers and underwater scenes, and one of Drew with his arm around a dark-haired beauty on the beach. The large kitchen diner at the back would be full of light in the daytime, and now it was cosy and inviting. A place where serious cooking and a lot of informal entertaining might take place. At the back, the kitchen lights illuminated a small garden, which was a riot of different shrubs, probably all planted with an eye to giving shelter and nourishment to different species of birds and insects.

He dumped her diving gear in the hall, and Caro followed him upstairs with the smaller bag that contained a change of clothes. The spare room doubled up as an office, with more books and a desk, and a pull-out sofa bed.

'I'll leave you to take a shower.' He jerked his thumb towards a door that led out to the top half of the kitchen extension downstairs and must be the bathroom.

'Thanks.' Caro couldn't suppress a yawn. She was rather hoping that Drew wouldn't want to talk too much now, because all she wanted to do was sleep.

'I'll make the bed up for you now. Would you like a hot drink before you turn in?'

'Um… Thank you. That would be lovely.' She couldn't stop herself from yawning again. A shower, a hot drink and then a comfortable bed sounded wonderful. Second only to curling up with Drew and falling asleep to the soft sound of his breathing, and neither of them were going to let that happen.

'Go, before you fall asleep in the shower.' He smiled, shooing her out of the room.

The warm water on her shoulder made it throb, and when Caro inspected it in the mirror there was a red mark that looked as if it was going to form into a bruise. The dolphin hadn't meant to attack her, she had just got in the way, and the damage was well worth the glimpse of the two dolphins circling the boats.

When she returned to the bedroom, the overhead light was off and a lamp burned by the bedside, throwing soft shadows across the room. The sofa bed was made up, with a warm blanket the colour of a stormy sea draped over the duvet. There was a folded T-shirt with the logo of the diving centre on the back, and Caro smiled, reckoning that this was Drew's way of telling her she'd earned her stripes as a diver. She towelled herself dry and slipped it over her head.

There was a mug with a saucer perched on top of it by the bed, and on further inspection it contained hot chocolate. Drew clearly wasn't expecting her to go back downstairs, and she slipped gratefully under the duvet. She'd only drunk half of the hot chocolate when drowsiness overtook her, and she snuggled down in the fresh-smelling sheets and closed her eyes.

It had been a while since Drew had cooked breakfast for more than one person. Sometimes it had just been him and Luna, and sometimes a whole gang of divers, who'd camped out in the spare bedroom and on the floor in the living room.

He'd woken early and rather than lie in his bed, staring at the ceiling and wishing that Caro was curled up next to him, he'd got up and gone downstairs. When he heard the quiet sounds of her moving around, and the noise of the shower, he started to make breakfast.

Twenty minutes later she appeared in the kitchen, her hair still damp and cascading down her back. Her eyes were bright, and she still had the last traces of a pillow crease in her cheek. Drew wondered if it was possible to kiss a pillow crease away and decided to view it only as evidence that she'd slept well.

Breakfast in company was different from the way he remembered it. Not the bandying of jokes and the hurried gulping down of coffee and bacon sandwiches, but Caro's warm eyes and a succession of questions and ideas, some of them completely crazy and a few that…if you just let go of your preconceptions they made every kind of sense. He forgot all about the insistent push to get out of the house and wanted to spend all day just talking to Caro, bathing in her unique and creative view of the world.

'Why not?' She shot him a laughing smile. *Why not* was the thing that marked Caro out from everyone else he'd ever known. She had a completely different set of boundaries from most people.

'Because… I don't know. I can't imagine sea life sending distress signals to us when something bad happens.'

'But what if they could? What if the dolphins are out there calling us right now? What if we just can't hear them? Or we *can* hear and we simply don't understand.' She took a bite from the slice of toast she'd been waving in the air to illustrate her point.

'What if that toast just shouted, *Don't eat me!*' He grinned at her.

She held the slice to her ear. 'Too late. I didn't hear it. But seriously, warning systems, Drew, triggered by the very organisms at risk. I'm sure that there are loads of surveillance systems in place for endangered species, but what if we could make them better?'

That was always Caro's refrain as well. Refusing to accept that some things were too hard or couldn't be made any better. She extended those principles to him, and her belief that he *would* heal had made him believe it too.

'I'm just a working vet…' Who didn't have the vision or the ability to turn far-fetched ideas into reality.

'Rubbish! You're the one who *gave* me the ideas in the first place.'

The thought that something he'd done had nudged Caro's creative process into gear and focussed her capricious mind was endlessly gratifying. Drew was still trying to get his head around it when his phone beeped, and he opened the text his father had sent.

'Dad says he's getting ready to go now. Is forty minutes too soon to meet him down at the harbour?'

Caro shook her head. 'I'm fine with that, if you are. Or sooner…'

There was still a lot more left to do. And Caro's drive and energy added a new facet to the task ahead of them. He nodded, texting his father that they'd be there as soon as they'd finished their coffee.

More birds. Not as many as yesterday, but a greater proportion of them were dead or dying. But every time they pulled a living bird from the water, and Drew laid it carefully in a makeshift nest in one of the boxes, he saw Caro give a little nod of pleasure.

There were more boats, too. As the day wore on, resources from various environmental agencies arrived, and Drew made his decision.

'I think we should go back in now. Tomorrow's going to be a busy day at the clinic, we'll be starting to clean the birds that are strong enough. There's not a lot more we can add here.'

They made their way back to the veterinary centre to drop off the boxes of birds, and then returned to the harbour at Dolphin Cove. He and Jake shook hands, wordlessly acknowledging the efforts of the last two days, and

Gramps came aboard, shooing Drew away when he offered to help tidy up on the boat.

'I'll take you home, then.' Drew loaded his and Caro's gear into the back of his car. She was beginning to look like a proper seafarer, clad in a thick sweater and oilskins and climbing off the boat without waiting for a helping hand. Gramps clearly considered this was all *his* doing and had exchanged a couple of jokes with her before he took up his usual stance, leaning against the helm and watching her go.

'Thank you. I guess I should go now while the tide's out.' She quirked her lips down, and it occurred to Drew that she didn't want to leave him, any more than he did her.

They had plenty of time, and he drove as slowly as he could to Smugglers' Top, without collecting a queue of other impatient drivers behind him. He parked on the rough ground that led down to the beach and opened the boot of the car.

'I'll give you a hand with your gear.'

'That's okay, I can manage. Although…' She hesitated. Drew could wait. 'Would you like to come up and have some lunch? You can catch the low tide again this afternoon.'

'Thanks, that would be great. Mum's reckoning on keeping Phoenix for a few days, so I don't have to get back for her.' Drew tried to sound casual about his reply.

'Right, then.' Caro gave him a delicious smile, picking up the larger and more cumbersome of the two bags and leaving the one that Drew could sling easily over his shoulder. 'You take that one.'

CHAPTER TWELVE

THE MORE THAT Drew did, the better he seemed. Caro had been reluctant to let him carry anything up the stone steps to Smugglers' Top, but she knew that Drew was just beginning to grasp at the reality of being able to do the things he wanted to. It would hurt him more to take nothing than it would to take the lighter bag.

All the same, he was limping a little when they got to the top. Caro unlaced her shoes, leaving them in the hallway, and made tea. Then she plumped herself firmly down on one of the sofas in the living area, propping her legs up on the cushions. Drew took the hint and did the same.

Once he was there, she could insist that he stay put while she cooked. Or...pulled something from the freezer to heat. The smell of part-baked bread, browning in the oven, made thick, chunky soup seem like more of a meal. When he stood again, to follow her back to the kitchen with his empty bowl, he walked without a limp, leaving his stick behind by the sofa.

'So what are you up to this afternoon? Working up some ideas?'

Maybe. If Drew left, she'd have nothing but her ideas to keep her company. She wondered if he knew how much he was a part of these latest ones. The way he listened and understood. The way he injected a note of practicality, without rejecting the blue-sky thinking.

'I'm just going to let them simmer for a while. Maybe I'll take a break.' Caro wondered if Drew could be persuaded to take a break with her.

'I'll leave you to it, then. I'd better make a move, the tide will be turning soon.'

Crunch time. Time to make sense of the last two days, when she'd felt closer to Drew than anyone else in her life. Time to wonder whether it was possible to create a compartment, away from her work and everything else, where there would be a bit of space for each other.

She watched as he fetched his shoes and sat down to lace them up. Then he picked up his stick… Maybe she should just let him go, but it seemed that he was taking all the air in the room with him. She was already feeling light-headed, and unable to think properly.

'Wait!' He'd pulled on his coat, and there was no time left to think. Just to act.

'What is it?'

Those blue eyes. The dark, slightly wayward curls that gave him an outdoors look even when he was indoors. The thought that someone like Drew couldn't really want her, and then the memory of his kiss, which led her to the inescapable conclusion that he did.

'I'm not very good at this.' She walked towards him.

'Don't sell yourself short. You're good at a lot of things.'

Yeah. Seduction wasn't one of them. Caro was a lot more comfortable when she said exactly what she meant, and meaningful glances weren't really her forte. Although strangely she always seemed to know exactly what Drew's meaningful glances meant.

'I want you to stay.'

His face softened. 'Because…?'

Drew wouldn't let her down. Not with this anyway. If he left, then he left, but he'd find a reason for doing so that wouldn't disappoint her. Something that probably wouldn't even hurt all that much.

'So that we can keep each other company tonight.' Caro congratulated herself on finding the words that made her meaning clear, without having to tell him exactly what she'd been imagining them doing together.

His eyes darkened suddenly. Pools of velvety black, with iridescent blue borders. So, so beautiful.

'It would be my privilege to keep you company to-night, Caro.'

Nice. That made her feel so good, and she wished she'd thought of saying something like that.

'But...' He twisted his mouth in an expression of regret.

Okay. There was a *but*. Maybe it was time to tell him that everything was okay and let him leave. His gaze fell to the stick in his hand, and his knuckles whitened against the curved top.

'My leg isn't... They say that with time it'll look a lit-tle better.'

He thought *that* was a problem? Caro had never really considered that Drew couldn't know how beautiful he was. With or without scars. She tapped the base of the walking stick with her foot, and it moved without any resistance. He wasn't actually leaning on it, and when she kicked it, it clattered to the floor.

'You're the kind of girl who would kick a guy's stick out from under him?' Drew's smile reflected her own hunger.

'Yes. You don't need it, Drew. And I couldn't care less what your leg looks like.'

Suddenly he reached for her, curling his arm around her waist and pulling her against him. When he kissed her, it was mind-blowing. Knee-shaking.

'Do you trust me?'

So he wanted trust. Any man would. Caro took a moment to think about her answer.

'I don't *not* trust you.'

He shook his head. 'That's not the same.'

'I trust you enough to go diving with you. And to want you to stay tonight.'

'And what *don't* you trust about me?' He tipped her chin with one finger, kissing her lips lightly.

'My work's always…something separate. I have to go wherever it leads me.'

He nodded, dropping kisses onto her neck. 'I understand that. We're very different people and I'm not sure that we'll ever be able to reconcile our lifestyles.'

That was a nice way of saying that she was a workaholic. Right now, none of their differences seemed to matter. Caro kissed him, and his response told her that it didn't matter to him either.

'I want to make love to you, Caro. For the rest of the afternoon and…then again this evening. And tonight…'

'That's enough, isn't it?' It would always have to be enough. Caro didn't know how to trust that a lover might truly become a part of her life any more.

'Right now, it feels more than enough.'

When he kissed her again, the ache for him went into overdrive, blinding Caro to everything else. He was slowly picking her apart, owning everything. It was so much more than just blinding physical pleasure this time because she knew that they understood each other.

'Can we go to the bedroom now?' She wanted the luxury of stretching out on the large bed, knowing that Drew wouldn't be struggling to balance.

He nodded. 'Then you can tell me exactly what's on your mind. And I'll tell you what's on mine.'

* * *

Drew couldn't believe this was happening. He'd wanted Caro from the first time he'd seen her. Had told himself that he couldn't have her. Known for sure that he couldn't have her, and then… She'd told him that she wanted him. And then they'd found a way to be together that didn't compromise either of them.

Her bedroom was all creams and neutral colours. The kind of room that took its only life from the people who were in it, and the colour of the sea and sky outside the large windows. The only piece of her was the stone he'd given her from the seabed, displayed proudly on the bed-side table.

She didn't rush him. He was still a little uncomfortable about the scars on his leg, and she didn't make a thing about him showing them before he was ready. She stripped off his coat and sweater, hurling them at a large wicker chair that stood in the corner. Then her own sweater, which missed the chair and landed on the floor. Caro took a little more time over his shirt, undoing one button at a time. They lay on the bed together, exploring all the subtly different ways that a woman could kiss a man and a man could kiss her back.

'Would you like to take a shower?' She ran her finger across his chest, and he felt a wake of sensation follow its path.

'And wash off the sea…?'

'No. I love the taste of salt on your skin. And your scent.' She trailed her tongue along the path that her finger had just taken, and Drew felt his whole body begin to stiffen. 'I'm giving a gentle hint that I want to see a little more of you. Maybe you want to see a little more of me?'

'I want to do more than just *see* a little more of you.'

She laughed, wriggling away from him off the bed,

and disappearing into the en suite bathroom. The sound of running water, and then she appeared in the doorway again. Naked.

'Come here…' He choked the words out.

'No. You come here.'

He was on his feet, pulling off his jeans and undershorts before he'd even thought about it. Her gaze dropped, but she clearly wasn't interested in his leg. That was okay, he wasn't embarrassed at showing her just how much he wanted her.

She let him watch as she soaped her body. It felt as if he should be on his knees before her, but it was Caro who bent to wash his legs, her fingers skimming over the scars as if they were of no consequence to her. He towelled her dry, kissing her at every opportunity, before he followed her back into the bedroom.

His knee twisted and he stumbled. Almost fell, before he grabbed at the footboard of the bed to steady himself. Suddenly he felt weak again, as if it had just been a fantasy that he could take back everything he'd once had.

Caro didn't make a move to help him. In fact, she moved back, swinging her legs up onto the bed and shifting to lean against the pillows.

'Hurry up, Drew…'

She didn't see him as weak or in need of any pity. Forgetting all about his leg, Drew slid onto the bed, pulling her towards him.

'You are so beautiful.'

'You don't need to say that.' She smiled, saying the words as if they didn't matter. She really didn't know… The thought that no one had ever made her feel any different cut him to the heart.

'I can't help it. Maybe you'll trust me enough to believe me before we're done.'

Her eyes widened in surprise. Soft and golden, and as gentle as a warm sea breeze. He kissed her, easing himself over her, his hand exploring the silk of her skin.

She didn't reply, but her gasp when his fingers found her nipple told him that he had her full attention. He wondered how long she could hold out against him and hoped it would be for just a little while.

He told her all of the ways that she was beautiful, all of the things he loved about her. Teased her until she was drunk with the same heady passion that intoxicated him.

'Drew. Please…'

He didn't want her to beg. He wanted her to receive him into her arms, knowing how much he adored her. Slowly he slid inside her, feeling the warm tension of her body.

Something stirred, deep in her eyes. He wrapped his hand around her leg, pulling it up and around his hips. His next thrust was a little faster, a little harder and she groaned.

Strength pulsed through him, unleashing a hurricane. There was no going back now. She was driving him beyond anything he'd ever experienced.

In the sudden calm, before the storm reached its height, he stared down into her eyes, and saw acceptance and trust. It was then that he knew that this was more than just passion. Caro was giving a part of herself to him, and he was giving whatever was left of himself to her.

Who had the stamina to work their way through half a box of condoms in sixteen hours? And who on earth could make things perfect and then manage to improve on that? Warmer and wilder, heart-thumpingly passionate and mind-blowingly intense.

And *then* make breakfast.

She watched him as he carried the tray over to the bed,

setting it down. Just jeans, slung low on his hips. The way he used those hips was just so satisfying.

'There *has* to be something wrong with you, Drew.'

He raised his eyebrows. 'Why's that?'

'Because you're too good to be true. You're the most beautiful man I've ever seen.' There was no denying that, she'd already told him. 'And you're gentle and very sweet, and I love it when you forget about both of those things…' She'd told him that too. In rather plainer terms than she could use this morning without blushing.

'Ah. You mean when you agreed with me that you were beautiful?' He sat down on the bed, and the plates and cups slid gently to one side of the tray.

'I think I said that was how *you* made me feel.' Caro was a little hazy on the exact details. Just that he'd coaxed something out of her that she hadn't know was there last night.

'I'd like to make you feel that again. If you'll let me.'

They hadn't talked about that. But it was impossible to deny that they both wanted it.

'I'd like that too.' She leaned forward to kiss him, and the contents of the tray tipped back the other way.

'My place? This evening? I'll go and pick Phoenix up from Mum's after work today.'

Caro had wondered whether his cottage might contain too many memories for Drew to make love with her there. It was also far less likely that an overnight visitor would escape notice in the village than it was here at Smugglers' Top.

'Don't you mind? If you feel better about coming here, I'm accessible via land or sea.'

He thought for a moment. 'No. I'd like it if you came to my place.'

Drew was moving on. She was glad for him, but something deep in Caro's heart sounded a note of warning. She'd moved out, and then moved away, but moving on was a little more difficult. But Drew had shown her how to do so many things, and maybe he could show her how to move on too.

'Okay. Your place tonight. I can come to the centre this afternoon to help out with the birds if you need me.'

'We're going to need all the help we can get. Thank you.'

'I'll see you around twelve, then. That'll give me the morning to work out what I need to do this week on the prosthetics project.'

He nodded, picking up the mugs from the tray and handing one to Caro, then taking a swig of coffee from the other. 'Okay, I'll leave you with the washing-up, then. I'd better get going.'

She ate her toast while he found his clothes and put them on. Then he kissed her, and Caro heard the front door close behind him.

Getting out of bed, she walked across to the bathroom, peering at her reflection in the mirror. All the things that Drew had said last night... She'd never really thought much about her looks, and Blake's betrayal had made her feel worthless and ugly. But she valued Drew's opinions much more than Blake's.

Her hair glinted in the overhead lights. Her eyes were marvels of evolutionary genius, but then so were everyone else's. There was nothing extraordinary about her features or her figure, but if you liked fair skin she supposed both were passable. And, last night, Drew had given her new respect for all her body was capable of. Perhaps, after all, she might accept that he *did* find her beautiful...

CHAPTER THIRTEEN

'YOU'RE LOOKING VERY pleased with yourself.' Ellie put the last of the birds that had been washed this morning in the drying pens. Drew had already perched himself on a stool, unable to stand any longer.

'Am I?'

'There you go again. Answering a question with a question never works, Drew.'

'You asked a question?'

Ellie puffed out an exasperated breath. 'All right, then. Dad said he was driving along the coast road early this morning, and he saw your car parked off the road by Smugglers' Top. He was concerned about you so he stopped to take a look, and he saw you walking across the beach.'

'Right. Does he have photographic evidence, or is this just word of mouth?'

'He said you were looking a bit furtive.'

'I was *not* looking furtive.'

'Ha! So you *were* there!' Ellie clapped her hands together. 'Can't I be a bit pleased for you, Drew? It's time you started dating again. And Caro's really nice, even if she can be slightly kooky at times.'

'Mostly that's just because she's thinking about something that's way over our heads.' Drew leapt to Caro's defence and Ellie shot him a knowing look.

'That's true. I really like her a lot, Drew. And she was
an absolute star, coming out with us to help with the birds.'

'Yes, well, she'll be coming in this afternoon to help
with cleaning them up. So don't start with her, Ellie. She
isn't used to everyone knowing her every move, she has a
normal person's expectation of privacy.'

'Of course I wouldn't say anything to make her feel
uncomfortable.' Ellie wrinkled her nose at him. 'And it's
good of her to come. You could do with a hand, the standing's a little too much for you.'

That and a couple of very gratifying positions last night.
Ellie really didn't need to know that.

'Yeah, you're right. I could use some help. But don't
start getting carried away, Caro and I are very different.
Like my mum and dad were, and you know as well as I do
what happened there. Caro has her work…'

'And that doesn't play out so well with you.' Ellie gave
him a knowing look.

Drew sighed. 'It's not going to get that far, Ells. We're
not really dating, we just have…a thing.'

Ellie nodded, suddenly leaning forward and planting
a kiss on his cheek. 'Well, I hope your *thing* makes you
happy. You deserve it, Drew.'

'Thank you. And if you want to get sloppy, go do it with
your husband. Lucas signed up for it when he married you.'

Ellie chuckled, poking her tongue out at him, the way
she used to when they were kids and flouncing out of the
room. Drew shook his head, Ellie wouldn't like the term
flouncing very much.

Caro *did* make him happy. And she'd told him that he
made her happy. They just had to be careful and remember that any commitment that they were tempted to make
wouldn't work.

And maybe he should try to look a little less happy

when he was at the clinic. Although with the prospect of Caro arriving in half an hour's time, that wasn't going to be easy.

It had been a long day. Actually, it hadn't been all that long, but it felt like it. Drew's leg was aching badly, and for the first time in a couple of weeks he'd taken the full dose of painkillers.

He'd wondered whether that would keep Caro away tonight. Maybe she didn't want to run around after him this evening while he sank down onto the sofa to rest. But when he'd hinted that maybe he should rest tonight, and she might like to go home, she'd given him a smile.

'Good. If you're resting, then I can cook for you.'

'What are you going to cook?' He'd never seen Caro cook anything. She was good at taking stuff out of the freezer and heating it up, and she was quite capable of working her way through a mountain of fruit and a stack of sandwiches at her desk, but cooking required leaving her workshop for more than ten minutes at a time.

'Anything you like.' She shot him a frown. 'That's what cookery books are for, Drew.'

'How about spaghetti Bolognese?' *Everyone* knew how to make that.

'Done.' She pulled her phone from her pocket. 'I'll find a recipe, and we can get the ingredients on the way home.'

'That's okay. I have the ingredients…'

When they got back to his cottage he spent a worrying forty-five minutes on the sofa, trying to tell himself that there was a limit to the amount of damage that one robotics engineer and a Labrador puppy could do in someone's kitchen. Caro appeared in the doorway, crooking her finger at him, and he levered himself onto his feet and followed her.

Phoenix ignored him completely in favour of the bowl of food that was laid out for her in the corner. The pans were all cleared away and in the sink. The blinds were drawn and the light over the dining table switched on. There were two plates of spaghetti Bolognese, a dish of grated Parmesan cheese, and a bottle of sparkling water on the table, along with a candle. The smell made his mouth water.

'Sit down.'

Drew regretted his doubts and did as he was told. Caro lit the candle and sat down, pouring the water into a couple of wine glasses while he sprinkled Parmesan cheese onto his food. She picked up her fork and he followed suit, aware that she was watching him.

The spaghetti was perfect. The sauce was wonderful. Drew rolled his eyes as he ate the first mouthful, prompting a smile from Caro.

'This is great. Really nice. Where did you get the recipe again?'

'I found four different ones. So I worked out what each element was supposed to achieve and chose the parts I liked the best.'

In other words, she'd applied the techniques she used in sorting and refining her own ideas. And it had all worked with the same apparent ease as her robotics projects.

'Well, you have to write it down. This is much better than my recipe.'

She gave him a luminous smile. 'You didn't think I could do it, did you?'

He should come clean and admit it. 'You don't cook all that much. I can see why, you get interested in something…'

'Yes, I know. I'm not working now, though.'

Maybe she could be persuaded to work a little less in

the future. Drew dismissed the thought. She was who she was, and just because that wasn't compatible with his way of life, it didn't give him the right to try and change her.

'You're as perfect when you're not working as when you are.' He decided on a compliment that covered both of their points of view.

'Thank you.' She waved her fork at him, grinning like a Cheshire cat. 'Eat. Before it gets cold.'

They spent the evening in the sitting room, Caro with her laptop balanced on her knees and Drew sprawled on the sofa with Phoenix. Drifting back and forth between talk and silence, ideas and thought. When Drew started to doze, she left him to sleep while she finished what she was doing and then closed her laptop, walking over to the sofa to shake him gently.

'Come upstairs if you want to sleep.'

'Uh. Yeah… Sorry.'

'Don't be. It's been a busy few days. You're not working tomorrow, are you?'

He thought for a moment. 'I may go in late.'

'That's a good idea. You have two jobs at the moment, and one of them is to heal.'

Drew sat up, and Phoenix jumped down off the sofa. Stretching, he got to his feet. 'Anything I can get for you? Before I tear off your clothes…?'

Tearing off her clothes sounded just fine to Caro. Now sounded even better. 'Where do you find the energy?'

'I have plenty of energy.' Drew looked wide awake now. 'My leg just gets in the way a bit sometimes.'

Drew had been an active and resourceful lover last night, but now he was hurting. He'd been forced to rest for so long now that all he wanted to do was shake off those constraints, but he was in danger of overdoing things.

'I have a solution. If you'd care to try it?'

'I'm *always* interested in your solutions…'

She followed him upstairs, and he caught her hand, leading her into the bedroom. Drew pulled her close, kissing her, and Caro backed him towards the bed, pushing him down onto it.

'I want you in full working order tomorrow, Drew. You've been overdoing things.'

'Whatever you say…'

'Seriously?'

He gave her a melting look. 'Seriously. I'm entirely in your hands.'

She'd hold him to that. She pulled off his sweater and shirt, started to undress him. Drew meanwhile had found something to do with his own hands, and they were skimming her body.

She wriggled free of him, backing away. Drew leaned back onto the bed, watching her as she undressed.

'I'm liking this *in your hands* business very much.'

'I can see…' Caro pulled back the bedspread, piling two pillows on top of each other. When she climbed onto the bed, flipping her finger towards them, he got the gist of what was expected of him and pulled himself backwards to lean against them.

'Is this where you tell me I won't feel a thing?' He grinned teasingly.

'I have reason to believe that you'll feel everything.' She grabbed a pillow from her side of the bed, propping it carefully under his knee. 'Comfortable?'

'Very. Thank you.'

His gaze followed her every move as she crawled slowly across the bed towards him. He reached up, caressing her cheek, and she felt him shiver as she climbed astride him.

'Caro, this is the best way of resting…'

She smiled, and saw his eyes darken suddenly. They both knew what came next, and the air itself seemed to be trembling with passion.

She bent down to whisper in his ear.

'Just lie back, sweetheart.'

Last night had been something else. Truly something else that owed nothing to the simple mechanics of great sex. Caro had taken him as he was and had turned caring into blinding, nerve-shattering passion.

He felt different. And, however much Drew told himself that this wasn't good, that he'd promised not to get so involved, he couldn't help it. Caro had captured his heart, and everything she did and said only made her hold on it more secure.

Ellie had called him early, not enquiring where he was or who he was with but telling him that he wasn't needed at the clinic today. Volunteers from local charities would be helping out with the birds, and the efforts of the environmental agencies in breaking down the oil slick were coming to fruition.

Drew knew that Ellie's assertion that there was *nothing for him to do* wasn't entirely true. He was sure he could find something, but it was clear that she and Lucas were managing. And in a perfectly co-ordinated pincer movement, Caro told him that she needed his help with the prosthetics project.

He spent the morning in her workshop, his leg propped up in front of him on the sofa. When Phoenix started to fret, jumping up onto the windowsill and pawing at the window, Caro told him to stay put, and that she'd take the puppy out for a couple of circuits of the small island.

Drew picked up the pieces of the prototype that Caro had been printing on the 3D printer, and which lay on her desk. He couldn't see how they fitted together, but there were notes and diagrams. He sat down, placing the pieces in order, and began to fathom how it would all work. He started to clip them together, and suddenly saw the concept clearly. It was simple but ingenious.

'What are you doing?' He hadn't heard Caro come in and he looked up to see her standing in the doorway of the workshop. Her face was like thunder, and he wondered what could have happened to make her so cross.

'I'm just taking a look at this. It's amazing…'

His words seemed to make her even crosser. 'Well, don't. You signed an agreement, remember?'

Okay. He remembered. But he still couldn't see why Caro was so angry. He put the pieces of the prototype back down on her desk.

'You do remember, don't you?' She wasn't going to let this go. 'Because I have a copy…'

'I remember. I'm sorry if I overstepped any boundaries.' Drew got to his feet. Annoyance was beginning to tug at him, but he didn't want to argue with her. Arguing never did any good.

'*Any* boundaries? You know just what the boundaries are, Drew. I told you that my work was separate from everything else and you said that was okay.' She seemed close to tears. 'You *don't* look at my work. It's mine, and I'll let you have the finished product when it's ready.'

'I'm trying to help, Caro. You asked for my help, remember?' He couldn't let this go.

'Yes, I asked you to *help*. I didn't ask you to go behind my back.'

Phoenix was sitting between them, looking back and forth, as if she knew that something bad was happening. Drew knew that something bad was happening, but he just couldn't work out what it was. Caro seemed to have changed so suddenly.

'All right. I'm not going to engage with this, Caro. We're both tired, and we probably need some space.' Drew wasn't sure that space was going to make any difference. But at least it ruled out any more conflict.

'I don't need any space, Drew. I just need you to understand.'

'Okay. Well, I'll go away and think about it. Maybe *you* should think about whether this reaction of yours isn't just a little bit paranoid.'

He turned, wondering if she might protest. All he heard was silence. He knew all about those silences, too. His parents had kept them up for days…

Drew grabbed his stick and called Phoenix, who bounded up to him as if she too wanted to get away from this. Clipping her lead onto her collar, he put on his jacket and walked out of the house without looking back.

This had been his mistake. He'd fallen for Caro, knowing that she was different from him. Knowing how committed she was to her work and knowing he couldn't change her. He should also have known that it was only a matter of time before the differences started to chafe, and the inevitable niggles turned into arguments.

Phoenix started to whine, pulling at the lead and pawing at the front door. 'No, Phoenix. We're not going back.'

The puppy gazed up at him. Phoenix didn't know about the bitterness of being let down, she was all trust.

The thing that had been niggling at the back of his mind suddenly became clear. He didn't understand, and he'd given Caro no chance to explain.

'Did it look as if she was about to explain, Phoenix?' He bent down stroking the puppy's head and she nuzzled against his hand. It was probably asking a bit much of a puppy to mediate between two grown people.

He could do better than this, though. He didn't need to walk away, maintaining the silence the way his parents had. If Caro was angry then she must have a reason, and he wanted to know what that was. Understand a little maybe.

He lifted the latch, pushing the front door with his finger. Caro clearly hadn't locked it behind him, and when the door drifted open a little he could hear the muffled sounds of her crying. That left him no choice. He had to go back and make things right. Even if he had to battle with Caro to do so.

CHAPTER FOURTEEN

IT HAD BEEN a surprise to see Drew sitting at her desk, handling her inventions. She'd reacted when she should have stopped and thought. But Drew was the one person that she'd thought would never betray her, and it had felt as if the bottom of her world had just fallen out.

It was too late now. Maybe he *had* intended to read through her notes behind her back for some reason. That wasn't the most likely evaluation of the situation. They'd shared so much already, and she'd never explained why sharing her work was such a touchy subject for her.

She'd messed up. If he had any sense, he wouldn't be coming back now.

'Caro…'

She almost jumped out of her skin. So much for Drew having any sense.

'I'm really sorry, Drew. You were right to go, and you should…just keep walking.'

'I'm not going to do that. I *want* to do it; I think you know why I can't deal with arguments. But that's my problem, not yours. So you can just throw whatever you want at me, and we'll take it from there.'

'I don't want to throw anything at you, Drew.' She couldn't look at him.

'That's fine too. I think I need to know why you reacted that way, though. I obviously hurt you, and I didn't mean to.'

'It's not your fault.'

'Maybe not. It'll be my fault if I walk away without finding out what's going on with you. So, if you don't mind, I'm just going to wait here until you think you can tell me.'

Phoenix bounded up to her, nudging and pawing at her legs, as if she hadn't seen Caro for months. Caro scrubbed at her eyes with her sleeve, remembering too late that it probably wasn't a great look.

She felt the sofa move as Drew sat down next to her, handing her a piece of kitchen roll from the kitchen. She tore it in half, blowing her nose with one piece and rubbing at her eyes with the other. He reached forward, smoothing down a lock of hair that was obviously sticking up and she turned the corners of her mouth down. She must look an absolute fright…

'You look beautiful.'

'What are you, a mind reader?'

'Sorry. Won't happen again.'

She reached for him, and his arms closed around her shoulders. The warmth of having him close only made her burst into tears again.

'I messed up, Drew.'

'Yeah. Me too.'

'I'm sorry.'

'So am I. Now tell me something I don't know.'

Caro heaved in a breath. It was time to face up to him and tell him the truth. He deserved that at least. She couldn't do this while she was still in his arms, so she sat up straight, looking into his eyes.

'It's not your fault, Drew, it's mine. It's…' Suddenly it

hit her. Drew wouldn't have treated her the way that Blake had. 'It's *not* my fault. I don't think it is anyway.'

'So tell me whose fault it is.'

'Blake. He taught at one of the universities I was associated with in California.'

'He was *your* teacher?' A note of concern sounded in Drew's voice.

Caro shook her head. 'If I'm honest, there wasn't a great deal that he could teach me.' This was new, too. She could see Blake from a different perspective now, and it didn't do him any favours.

'Okay. More a colleague, then. To be honest, that doesn't sound quite so inappropriate on his part.'

He knew. He'd put two and two together and realised that no one could hurt you as much as someone you loved. That was why Caro had been so afraid when she'd seen Drew looking at her work.

'I thought he loved me. I loved him, and I thought I'd found my home with him. I shared all my ideas and...' Caro shook her head miserably.

'He took them from you?'

'Worse. When the water feature in our garden kept getting gunked up I developed a self-cleaning valve. He patented it, and I lost the rights to it, which meant I couldn't develop it any further and make it available free in developing countries. He didn't steal it from me, he stole it from all the people who might have benefited from it.'

'What did he do with the patent?'

'He tried to sell it. There was a lot of interest and he was set to make a life-changing amount of money from it. He told me that I was stupid, and that someone had to look after my business affairs for me.'

'Wait. No, Caro. Anyone who ever tells you that you're stupid...well, that reflects on them and not you.'

'Trusting him wasn't my finest hour...'

'Someone deceived you. That doesn't make you stupid.' Drew shook his head. 'Is there anything you can do to claim the patent back?'

'I was so embarrassed. I left him and put the whole thing in the hands of an attorney in the States. She's trying to get the patent transferred to a charity that will do the right thing with it, and it looks as if she'll succeed. I just... I can't get any closure from that, Drew. I just wanted to crawl away and hide. Forget about it all.'

'But you can't, can you?'

Caro sighed. 'I think that's pretty self-evident, don't you?'

'Okay. I'm going to take this as a compliment.'

She stared at him. 'How do you work that one out?'

'You were afraid that it was all happening again. That someone you cared about would betray you. To jump to that conclusion, and react so strongly, means that you must care about me.'

'That's...one way of looking at it. I *do* care about you.'

'And I imagine it's not so easy to trust me after what happened.'

'I'm working on it.'

He pulled her close, kissing the top of her head. 'Yeah, I'm working on a few things too. Neither of us is perfect.'

'What are we doing together, then?' The obvious question didn't make her feel any better.

He chuckled. 'Well, for my part, you're probably the most interesting person I've ever met. You're very clever, and you're beautiful and a good person. And the sex is amazing.'

'I thought it was just me who thought the sex was amazing.' She grinned at him.

'Then you haven't been listening to me. What do you like about me?'

'All of the above. And you have a really cute puppy.'

Drew nodded. 'Yeah. The cute puppy does it every time. Why do you think I have her?'

There was something she had to do, even if it did still frighten her a little. Caro slid away from him, getting to her feet. 'I want to show you, Drew. All of my designs and sketches. The way the prosthetic's going to work.'

He caught her hand, holding on tight. 'No. I don't want to see it. Not until you've finished and it's under licence.'

'But… I want to show you that I trust you.'

'I know, and I appreciate that. Let's just take what we have for the time being, Caro. Know that there are things we can't reconcile yet, and that maybe that will change.'

'Hang on in there until it does, you mean.'

'Yeah. I'm definitely hanging onto you.' He pulled her down onto his lap.

It wasn't everything, but it was something. Something to hope for when Caro had lost hope completely.

'So, while we're hanging on… I don't suppose there's any hope of some more of that amazing sex, is there?'

'Not a chance.' He rolled her over on her back, kissing her. Just as she was starting to melt into what promised to be the greatest make-up sex ever, a shape moved on the periphery of her vision.

'Drew. Drew! We have to go to the bedroom, Phoenix is *watching*…'

'Can you feel it?' Drew's voice sounded behind Caro.

'No. I can't feel anything. Apart from deep mistrust.'

'Just relax. Let your shoulders do the work.'

Caro pulled on the oars. This wasn't as easy as Drew

made it look. The boat seemed to be going backwards, not forwards.

'You've got stronger shoulders than me.' Her tone sounded unpleasantly whiny. This rowing business was bringing out the worst in her.

She felt him slide forward, planting his feet on either side of her and his hands next to hers on the oars. *That* was better. She could feel the raw power of his body against hers, and when he pulled on the oars the boat started to make some headway.

'Now can you feel it?'

'Yes. Wonderful.' She relaxed against his chest.

'I meant the tide.'

'Oh. No, I think I'll have to practise a bit more. Maybe when I'm a bit less tired.'

His lips brushed against her neck as he planted a kiss. *That* she'd definitely felt. 'Why don't you go and sit with Phoenix?'

Phoenix was sitting in the stern, wearing her red life-jacket, her nose aloft in the evening breeze. Caro slid forward, careful to keep to the centre of the small craft as she turned around.

'That's much better. I can watch you row.'

He grinned at her. 'I get it. You like watching me work.'

'Yes, I do actually. You make an excellent reindeer wrangler.'

Drew pulled on the oars. 'I wasn't wrangling. I was attempting to hold them still while I did their health checks. And you didn't do so badly yourself.'

Caro chuckled. 'Apart from when I fell flat on my face in the mud.'

'You're particularly delightful when you're covered with mud.'

It had been a good day. Drew had suggested that Caro

might like to come with him to see the reindeer, and he'd let her help hold the animals while he gave them a thorough examination. They'd gone to the Hungry Pelican for supper and ended up missing the tide. Caro had a video conference booked with a robotics researcher in Australia first thing in the morning, so Drew was rowing her home.

'I can see why you like it. The sea. It makes you feel that the little things don't matter so very much.'

He nodded. 'Yeah. It's been here so much longer than we have. And it's so much bigger than us.'

'You must have missed it. When you were in hospital.' Drew loved the open skies, whether they were on land or sea. Being cooped up in bed for so long must have been hard on him.

'It was the worst thing...' His face darkened. 'Almost the worst anyway.'

Maybe she shouldn't ask. But talking about the bad things with Drew had helped her to begin to come to terms with them.

'What was the worst?'

He shook his head. 'You don't want to hear that, do you?'

'Yes. I do, actually. Whatever it was, it doesn't frighten me.'

The water slopped against the side of the boat as he pulled silently on the oars. There were a lot of things that he hadn't said about the accident, and sometimes his flat assurances to everyone that he was okay and doing well seemed more for their benefit than for his.

'When I ran the car off the road, I was alone.' He spoke suddenly. 'I was dazed at first, and my leg didn't hurt all that much. The pain came later.'

'You were in shock.' Caro nodded him on. Drew needed

to say this and injecting her own sense of horror into the mix wasn't going to help him.

'Yeah. It was very quiet, and I could hear a dripping sound. I could feel blood seeping through my clothes, and...' He stopped rowing suddenly, leaning on the oars as the boat bobbed up and down. 'I knew that if someone didn't come soon, I'd die.'

'So you held on.'

'I'm not entirely sure that it made any difference. But, yes, I willed myself to live. And I willed whoever happened to drive past to see my car and stop.' He shrugged. 'I've never told anyone that. Everyone assumes that I was unconscious, and I don't remember.'

'I've heard that a lot of people don't remember.'

He nodded, started to row again. 'Yes, I've heard that too. It didn't work that way for me.'

She hugged Phoenix as the boat moved forward in the water. Caro waited for him to say more, but it seemed that Drew had said everything that was on his mind.

'Thank you for telling me.'

'Thank you for listening.' He smiled suddenly. 'I appreciate you not handling me with kid gloves. Probably a great deal more than you know.'

Blake hadn't appreciated it at all. He had always been telling her that she shouldn't be so literal, or so outspoken. But then Blake, and all his put-downs, were right where they ought to be. A long, long way away.

'I could do kid gloves. If I put my mind to it.' Caro covered Phoenix's ears with her hands, and Drew chuckled. He knew what that meant. 'Tonight...'

'Sex with kid gloves. How does that work?'

'I touch you very slowly. *Very* gently.' Caro smiled at him.

'I'm up for that. And leave Phoenix's ears alone, she doesn't know what we're talking about.'

'She knows some things.' Caro spelled out the word *cheese*.

'Okay. Well, if you don't associate the word *sex* with treats from the fridge, then it's not likely to have much significance for her...' He manoeuvred the boat carefully into mouth of the cave beneath her house. Together they pulled it out of the water, then Drew wrapped his arms around her and kissed her.

'You, on the other hand, react very admirably to the word...' she whispered in his ear, feeling his body harden against hers.

Drew chuckled. 'Just goes to show how well you're training me up.' His fingers brushed the side of her face, so lightly that it made Caro shiver. She took his hand, leading him through the cavern and into the house.

Drew struggled to think of a time when he'd been so happy. There had been odd instances, but he'd never before been so perfectly content for twenty-one consecutive days.

It was odd. Nothing was settled between him and Caro. They were still different, and their relationship still wasn't going anywhere. But happiness didn't listen to logic, it just burst in on his heart anyway.

They tramped every inch of the ten acres around the Dolphin Cove Veterinary Clinic. They went beachcombing and diving in the bay. Drew showed her the woods, and the badger setts, and they listened in the silence for birdcalls. Phoenix seemed to be growing in front of his eyes and was developing an even bigger appetite and a gentle but mischievous nature. And he was getting stronger. His leg still hurt from time to time, and would do for a while, but he was beginning to feel powerful and able to tackle anything again.

They shared their nights, and when Drew wasn't working at the clinic he spent his days with Caro. She still maintained a fearsome work schedule, but Drew could make sure that she ate something by cooking for her while she worked. And coaxing her to bed was never that difficult.

He was falling in love. And love brought with it the terror of loss. Drew tried hard not to think about it, because he knew in his heart that he couldn't overcome his fears, and they had the power to tear them apart.

Yesterday she'd finished the first prototype of her animal prosthetic, and they'd packed it into a box and taken it to the clinic. Lucas and a selected group of consultants would be putting it through a whole barrage of tests, and assessing its viability, and he and Caro could take the weekend off. Drew had made cupcakes with candles to celebrate.

It wasn't unusual for him to wake up alone. Caro often got up early, and he'd find her pottering around in her workshop, still wearing her pyjamas. But when he went to find her, calling that he was about to make coffee, she didn't reply. And when he looked out of the window he saw something that almost made his heart stop.

Throwing on his clothes, he rushed down the steps onto the beach.

'Caro! Get out of the water!'

She was wearing her drysuit and had waded into the sea until it was up to her waist. The brisk autumn breeze and a strong tide was buffeting her back and forth, so that she could hardly keep her footing, and a snorkel hung from her hand. Much good that would do her in this rough sea—she was just as likely to get a lungful of water as she was air.

'In a minute.'

'Now, Caro!'

She turned, pulling a face at him. And then the unthinkable happened, and a wave crashed into her back, knocking her off balance. Sudden panic gripped Drew's heart and he waded into the water.

'All right…' She was thrashing around, trying to regain her footing. 'I can manage.'

She couldn't. She splashed around a bit more, buffeted by the tide and weighed down by the heavy suit, and finally she stopped fighting him and accepted his help. Drew marched her out of the water, trying to quell his anger.

'I was just getting what I wanted, Drew.' She brandished the underwater camera that Jake had lent her from the diving centre, and for a moment Drew cursed Jake for being so accommodating.

'What was so important that you had to go into the water anyway?'

'Those little crabs that we saw the other day. I was thinking about the way they scatter and react, and I wanted to see if I could work out a pattern.'

'And you couldn't wait one second longer and ask me to go with you? You know how strong the tide is on this beach, and there's a riptide further along here…' The mere thought made him feel sick.

'Yes, you told me about that last week. It's fine here, the tide was a little stronger than I'd thought, but I was managing.'

'Managing isn't good enough. You know that.'

He needed to calm down. If he could just get off the beach, then maybe the feeling of nauseous panic at the risk that Caro had taken might subside a bit, and he could reason with her. Drew turned, walking back up the steps to the house, and he heard the swish of the drysuit as she followed him.

Caro marched into the bathroom, leaving a trail of water behind her and slamming the door. Drew's overnight bag was in the bedroom and he grabbed a set of dry clothes from it, bundling the wet ones into a ball and shoving them back into the bag.

Yes, he was overreacting. And, no, he wasn't going to apologise for it. He of all people should know the dangers. And Caro knew why he couldn't compromise on safety and had always accepted that.

She was in the bathroom for a long time. Drew suspected that she was spending most of it cursing him. It would probably be best to wait and talk about this when they were both a bit calmer.

A bit calmer wasn't going to happen any time soon. Drew told himself that this was just a matter of her safety. That was of primary importance, but he knew that it was more than that. Their increasing intimacy was as challenging to Caro as it was to him. And they were both reacting in the only ways they knew how.

She made coffee in silence. They sat in silence to drink it and finally she got to her feet, making for the door that led to her workshop.

'Don't, Caro…' If she disappeared in there, she'd be lost to him until this evening at least. He'd be cooling his heels, rehearsing all of the things he needed to say to her, and that wasn't going to make things any better.

'What, then? Drew, you're not in charge of what I do.'

'No, but I'm asking you to come back here and sit down.'

She did it, but not without a sulky quirk of her lips. Drew ignored it and tried to organise his thoughts a little. Maybe see things her way.

'Caro, I know that your work is important to you. It's been your home and your companion when you didn't have anyone. But I can't watch you put yourself at risk like this.'

She thought for a moment. 'Going out on my own was a stupid thing to do, I'll admit that. But I didn't *mean* to take risks. I just…got an idea and…you know how it is, Drew. I don't think about anything else.'

'What I see is that you don't trust me. I get too close, and suddenly you're hiding behind your work. It's all-consuming, Caro, and I can't just stand aside and watch you working every hour of the day and night just to protect yourself from me.'

Drew shook his head. He'd thought that if they talked about this rationally, they'd find some solution. But all he'd done was convince himself that it would never work between them.

'I'm not sure I know how to do things differently.' Her eyes softened suddenly. 'I'm not very good at trusting people.'

'I know that, and I understand. But you have to understand how I feel.'

'Yes. I do.'

And that wasn't going to make any difference. He could never change Caro, and he didn't want to. He didn't know how to change himself either.

They stared at each other for a long time. When a tear ran down her cheek it almost broke him.

'I'm going to go.' Perhaps she'd say something that would allow him to stay. Give in just a little. But he knew she couldn't.

'You must do whatever you need to do, Drew. I won't ask you to stay.'

She *couldn't* ask him to stay. Caro knew all about moving on, and next to nothing about staying.

There were still a few more moments to turn this around. He called Phoenix and clipped her lead onto her collar. Put his jacket on, taking his time to zip it up. But there was nothing he could possibly say to stop the tide that was carrying them irrevocably away from each other.

Goodbye would hurt too much. *I'll see you* would be a lie. Drew didn't even dare take a last look at her, because he knew she'd be crying, and he doubted he'd be able to stem his own tears. He closed the front door behind him, and this time he wasn't going back.

CHAPTER FIFTEEN

CARO WAS EXPECTING LUCAS. She'd also expected to be up and dressed by the time he arrived, but last night she'd been up late, working. She hadn't made any progress, but it had been better than lying awake, missing Drew, the way she had every night for the last two weeks. Somehow work didn't seem to ease the pain the way it always had before.

The doorbell rang, and she grabbed her oversized cardigan, pulling it on before she went to answer it. Ellie was looking fresh faced and fabulous on the doorstep, a cardboard box tucked under one arm. That was the last thing she needed.

'Ellie… Sorry. Bit of a late night last night.'

Ellie nodded. 'Yeah, I was in my pyjamas until about half an hour ago.'

She was being nice. Extra nice, in fact, because Drew was Ellie's friend, and Caro was on the outside now. She stood back from the doorway, and Ellie grabbed Mav's hand, leading him inside.

'Where *did* you get those?' Ellie gestured towards her blue and green pyjama bottoms. 'I love them, I have to have a pair.'

'Uh…in America. I'll look up the web link, maybe they have an online shop.' And then what was she going to do? Write to Ellie as if she was her friend, with a shopping link? Ellie was hiding it well, probably for Mav's sake, but she'd be justified in wanting to scratch Caro's eyes out.

'I brought your prototype back. Lucas and the review committee's response is in here as well.' Ellie handed Caro the box.

'Thanks.' Ellie perched the box on top of the packing cases in the hall.

'I'm afraid they've suggested a few changes.' Ellie grimaced apologetically.

'That's fine. It's exactly what I wanted them to do. This is the first step in a long process, and it'll be a while before I get it exactly right.'

Mav was looking up at her expectantly, and Caro remembered the promise she'd made to Lucas. She bent down, plastering a smile onto her face. 'Would you like to see what I've got for you?'

'Yes!'

'Please.' Ellie provided the missing word. Caro hurried into her workshop, bringing out the box she'd saved for him.

The little tortoises were now little crabs. And there were some programming modifications, which meant that their movements weren't controlled just by proximity to anything else in their path. These had an additional interaction with each other.

'Here you go.' She put the box down on the floor next to the coffee table. Mav reached in, taking out a crab and finding the *on* switch without being told. That was one of the reasons why Caro had offered the crabs to Lucas for Mav to play with. Kids weren't fazed by the complexities of technology, they just tried things out.

'If you're busy, Caro…' Ellie watched as Mav took the crabs out of the box, one by one, switching them on and setting them onto the table.

'That's okay.' Caro shrugged. 'Actually, it would be very interesting to see how Mav interacts with them. I've introduced social and group behaviours into their programming.'

Ellie looked at her blankly and then grinned, walking over to Mav and pulling his coat off, while her son ignored her completely, already fascinated by the movement of the crabs. 'I don't entirely understand what you just said. But thanks.'

'Would you like some coffee?'

'Love some. You see to Mav, I'll make it.' Ellie slung her coat onto the back of a chair and marched into the kitchen, disregarding the plates in the sink and the breadcrumbs on the worktop, and switching the coffee machine on.

She could almost see Mav's mind working, the way he was trying things out with the crabs and learning their behaviour. It was a project in itself, and Caro wondered if she might borrow him for a couple of hours, just to observe. Probably not. Ellie wouldn't want her around him too much, and if Mav knew that she'd hurt his beloved Uncle Drew he'd be throwing the crabs at her instead of playing with them.

'Milk and sugar?' Ellie's voice interrupted her reverie.

'Um… Just a little milk, please.' Caro walked over to the breakfast bar as Ellie sploshed the milk into the cups.

She had to say *something*. 'Ellie, I appreciate your coming.'

Ellie looked up at her, a trace of knowingness in her eyes. 'What do you mean? We really appreciate you allowing Mav to play with your little robots.'

'I suppose… I meant I appreciate you coming and not trying to beat me over the head with a frying pan. I'm assuming you're not saving that for later…' Caro climbed on one of the high stools and pulled her coffee towards her.

Ellie pursed her lips. 'Look, Drew's my friend. More than my friend, you know he's like a brother to me. I know that he wouldn't want me to take sides, and I have no interest in that either. The one thing I've learned with Lucas is that there are always two sides to everything.'

'That's…good of you.' Caro shifted awkwardly in her seat. 'How is Drew?'

'Oh, like a bear with a sore head. I offered him my services as a vet, I've never treated a bear before, but I could give it a go. He turned me down, though.' Ellie shrugged. 'He knows that Lucas and I are both there for him.'

'Good. That's good.' Caro wondered if she should thank Ellie for looking after Drew, but she'd given up the right to do that. Ellie and Lucas were his friends, of course they looked after him.

'How are you?'

'Um. Keeping busy.'

Ellie plonked herself down on one of the stools on the other side of the breakfast bar. Clearly Caro's answer wasn't the one she was looking for, but Caro hadn't been doing much else other than missing Drew and keeping busy. She took a sip of her coffee, hoping that Ellie might drop the subject.

No such luck. 'Those crates in the hallway…?'

Caro heaved a sigh. 'I was thinking of going back to Oxford. I can continue with my work on the prosthesis there.'

'I imagine it would be good to be near the university.' Ellie was gazing at her thoughtfully.

'Yes. It would.'

That wasn't the reason. Caro was cutting and running. As a child, she'd learned that looking back never worked, and she'd applied the same principles with Blake when he'd broken her heart, putting as much space between them as she could. Now she was doing it again with Drew because it was the only thing she knew how to do.

'Look, Caro, it's none of my business...'

'That's okay.' Cruel hope flashed into Caro's heart. Maybe Ellie had seen something that neither she nor Drew were able to.

'Drew's miserable. And from what I can see, so are you.' Ellie held up her hands in a gesture of appeasement. 'And if you don't want to be with him, that's your business and you should tell me to take my nose out of it. But he's a good man.'

'Yeah, I know. He's the best.'

Ellie nodded. 'I don't know what he's thinking, he hasn't talked to me. But I'll take a guess that he wouldn't want you to leave because of him.'

What did *that* mean? Caro shot Ellie a questioning look and she shrugged. Ellie obviously didn't know either, she was just making an observation.

But the seed was sewn, and Caro's heart was fertile ground for it. Her parting with Drew had been final, they'd both wanted it that way. But she still loved him. She had no choice but to trust him and stay a little longer. She had to wait for him.

'I... I do like it here. There's something about Dolphin Cove.'

'I think so too.' Ellie smiled. 'Why don't you at least come down to the Hungry Pelican one evening with me and Lucas? I can get Drew to babysit, so you won't be bumping into him unexpectedly.'

It was kind of Ellie to ask. Caro had no intention of taking her up on the offer, however much she wanted to.

'Thanks. Maybe...when things have blown over a bit?'

'Whenever you want.' Ellie nodded, grinning. 'Look, if you're not doing anything this morning, why don't you

go and get dressed, and give Mav a hand with those little
monsters over there? I'll do the washing-up.'

'No!' Caro looked over at the plates in the sink and felt
her ears redden. 'You're not doing my washing-up.'

Ellie laughed. 'Nonsense. You should see how much
washing-up Lucas and Mav generate, this is child's play.
Go and get dressed and maybe we'll go down to the beach
and see how they work on sand.'

Drew had finally come to a conclusion. He'd raged over the
fact that he couldn't change, and Caro couldn't either, for
three weeks now. He'd been tight-lipped and grumpy with
everyone at the clinic, even telling Tegan off for painting
her nails in the reception area. When he'd gone back to
apologise to her for his show of temper, Tegan had smiled
sweetly at him and done her best to console him with the
latest action pictures of her horse. Drew appreciated it
but it was better to just keep his distance from everyone,
Lucas and Ellie included.

He'd shut himself away from everyone when he hadn't
been working and had stewed on his own in a slow bubble
of anger flavoured increasingly with despair. And then
he'd made his decision.

If Caro wanted him, even half as much as he wanted her,
then they could work something out. He didn't know how,
but maybe he could convince her to at least talk about it.

He took a couple of hours off work and drove into
Penzance, without thinking about why he was making
the trip. He wandered past shop windows, without properly knowing what he was looking for. But when he saw
the ring in the jeweller's window, he knew that this was
exactly why he was here.

It was a platinum eternity ring, with blue-green em-
eralds inlaid all the way around it. When he went inside

and asked to see it, the colours flashed and changed like the sea. Like the ever-moving, ever-fascinating workings of Caro's mind.

'What size would you like, sir?'

That was a problem. Drew brushed it away. 'I'm not sure. Her hands are about the same size as yours, does it fit you?'

The assistant flashed him an uncertain look, but she tried the ring on anyway. Drew tried to imagine it on Caro's hand, and the comparison didn't really work for him. This was Caro's ring, and she was the only one who should wear it.

'I'll take it.'

'It would be better if you could find out the size. This is a lovely ring, but it isn't easy to resize something of this design. It's a lot of expense to go to if you're not sure.'

That was the least of Drew's worries. He wasn't sure whether Caro would even accept the ring. Or which finger she'd wear it on if she did. For the moment, all he could think was that he'd keep it in his pocket as a reminder. An expression of intent.

'That's okay.'

The assistant hesitated. He wondered if he should ask to speak to the manager and complain that that an assistant who wouldn't sell him what he wanted wasn't doing her job properly. Actually, she was doing her job very well, and this was madness.

'Please. This is the ring I want.'

'All right. If you bring it back undamaged within the next fourteen days, we'll give you a credit note.'

The assistant put the ring into the box and started to wrap it. Drew found himself smiling at her and realised he'd been under-using those muscles recently.

He drove back to the clinic and spent the rest of the

morning and the better part of the afternoon in his consulting room. Somehow the stream of patients didn't seem quite so daunting when he knew that the ring was in his pocket. Drew didn't think about what he was going to do with it, or whether he was going to get a chance to do anything with it. For the moment it was enough that it was there.

When he walked out of the clinic that evening, the air seemed fresh and clean. He wandered down towards the beach, slipping his hand into his pocket and tracing the shape of the ring with his fingers. As the waves lapped against the sand, he stared out towards the horizon. The view here was ever changing and yet still always the same.

Suddenly he knew. It had been staring him in the face, and he hadn't seen it. Now that he did, Drew realised that the answer had been obvious all along. He turned, making for his car. He had to hurry; he had a tide to catch...

Caro was no particular stranger to crazy ideas, but this had to be the craziest yet. Sitting on the bench that overlooked the open sea, as the sun fell in the sky. She told herself that she was appreciating the view and getting a breath of fresh air, but when she closed her eyes all she could see was a light, fixed in the prow of a small rowing boat. Drew, pulling strongly on the oars, coming for her.

The longing to see him became sharper each day. Sometime soon it would be stronger than the fear of rejection, the dread of what he might say. Until then, she'd wait for him.

This evening, he seemed so real. She could almost hear his voice, calling her name...

'Caro...!'

She almost jumped out of her skin. That actually *was* Drew's voice. Or maybe she was just going completely mad. Caro sprang to her feet, whirling around, and saw a dark shape walking slowly towards her.

'Drew?' A shiver down her spine accompanied the thought that he couldn't really be here at all. 'How did you get here? The tide's coming in...'

He was closer now. Clearer in the failing light. 'I had to wade out to the steps.'

Caro's gaze fell to the watermarks on his trousers, just above his knees. He *had* come. Not the way she'd imagined, but he'd come and that was all that mattered.

She swallowed hard, trying not to allow false hope to take root. 'Why are you here, Drew?'

That smile. The one he always gave when she got straight to the point. It was just one of the things she'd been dreaming about...

'Caro, I've walked out on you twice. If you can find it in your heart to take me back, I promise you that I'll never do it again.'

A tear rolled down her cheek and she brushed it away impatiently. 'I was waiting for you, Drew.'

He stepped forward, and Caro saw that he was trembling, as if he was afraid to touch her. But when she flung herself into his arms he was there, so solid and unmistakeably real, and hugging her tight.

'I kept you waiting for too long...'

'It doesn't matter. You're here now.' She snuggled into his arms. 'You told me that I was hiding behind my work and you were right. But I've changed. I trust you, and I want to be with you.'

'I've changed too, Caro. I was wrong when I said that it wasn't possible, because loving you has changed me. I want to be with you, and I'll do whatever it takes to make you happy. Go wherever you go—'

'I don't want to go anywhere, Drew. I like it here.'

'Really? You're not just saying that, are you?'

'When did I ever *just say* things? I love it here, Dolphin Cove and the Hungry Pelican, the reindeer...' She hugged him tight. 'And you. I love you most of all.'

'Then you give me no choice.' He sank to one knee, flashing her a delicious smile.

'I love you, Caro, completely and wholeheartedly. Please marry me.'

For a moment she thought she was going to collapse under the sheer weight of joy. Tears sprang to her eyes, and Caro could only manage one word. But it was the word that mattered.

'Yes...'

He caught his breath, pulling her close. If he'd only stand up now she could kiss him properly. But Drew was feeling in his pocket, his other hand finding hers.

'Yes, Drew... Yes.' She wanted to say it again.

'I heard.' He grinned, holding out a ring that sparkled in the half-light. Caro couldn't see it properly through her tears, but it didn't actually matter. If he'd chosen to tie a piece of string around her finger, she'd treasure it.

They both gasped as he slid the ring onto her trembling finger. Caro pulled him to his feet, kissing him. Everything...*everything* was all right now. They'd made it right.

Drew took her hand, looking at it as if to check that he hadn't been dreaming and that the ring was still there. It *was* gorgeous.

'It's beautiful, Drew. And it fits me. How did you know what size to get?'

'I didn't. The shop assistant tried to talk me out of buying it.'

Caro wrapped her arms around his neck. 'And they say *I'm* crazy.'

'This is the sanest thing I've ever done.'

'Mmm. Me too. Got any ideas about our next sane and logical step?' She was sure he would.

He wrapped his arms around her shoulders. 'Since we're engaged to be married now, I think the least you could do is ask me in for a coffee.'

Caro chuckled. 'I think I should get you out of those wet clothes. *Then* make you coffee.'

'Let's forget all about the coffee, shall we?'

She clung to his hand, pulling him towards the house. The front door slammed shut behind them and they abandoned their coats and shoes in the hallway. There was no time for anything else but kisses.

'Oh!' Caro gasped as he lifted her off her feet, walking purposefully towards the bedroom. 'Be careful…'

'It's all right.' He was limping a little but his leg held firm. They'd already made the greatest journey, and now it was just a matter of a few steps.

EPILOGUE

Eight months later

ELLIE SEEMED VERY CALM. Annoyingly so. She also looked immaculate, in the way that only Ellie could with the breeze tugging insistently at her riot of curls.

'You're sure you don't want a sea sickness tablet? I've got some in my bag.' Ellie brandished the small, embroidered drawstring bag that she had looped around her wrist.

'No, I'll be fine. I always feel sick on boats for the first five minutes, and then it wears off.'

'You're sure about that?'

No. Caro wasn't sure about anything at the moment. Whether Drew would really want to get married on a boat. Whether being pregnant would tip the balance and mean that she was going to be sick all over her wedding dress...

She looked out to sea, taking deep breaths. Thinking of Drew's smile calmed her, because she knew that Drew would be waiting for her, and that he wanted today as much as she did. He wanted the rest of their lives as much as she did.

Gramps climbed aboard, looking dapper in his suit, and planted a kiss on Caro's cheek. 'You look beautiful, lass. Are you ready?'

'I'm ready, Gramps.'

'Then we'd better get going before the lad decides he's not going to wait any longer.'

'Gramps!' Ellie protested. 'Don't say that!'

'We'll find out soon enough.' Gramps waited for Peter and Diana to board, then started the engine, manoeuvring the boat away from the dock.

Drew would wait for her however long it took, Caro knew that without question. The sea was glittering in the sunshine, and the day was going to be perfect. As the boat sailed out of the tiny port of Dolphin Cove, she felt the queasiness in her stomach subside.

Drew had stayed the night with Ellie and Lucas in their apartment above the veterinary centre. Ellie had left at the crack of dawn to help Caro with her dress and the final arrangements for the wedding, both of which Caro had managed to keep secret from him.

He was already happier than he'd ever thought he could be. When they'd found out that Caro was pregnant, they'd decided to bring their wedding day closer, and Caro had told him that she wanted to surprise him and organise everything. She'd been making furtive phone calls for the last three weeks, and Ellie and Lucas's flat had become a no-go area for him, their spare bedroom having been given over to mysterious *things for the wedding.*

At eleven o'clock Lucas had announced that it was time to go, and chivvied him and Mav down to the deserted beach.

'Okay. So we're here. Now what?'

'Wait and see.' Lucas was looking annoyingly smug.

'Mav…?'

Mav shrugged. 'I don't know. No one told me.'

That was probably just as well. Mav wouldn't have been

able to keep the secret, so he and Drew had both been kept in the dark.

'You've got the rings, though. Tell me you have the rings, Lucas.'

'Yes, I've got the rings. Simmer down, mate.'

That was one thing sorted at least. Lucas would be giving Caro away, and Ellie had agreed to be Drew's best man, on condition that *this* best man was going to be wearing a dress. Mav had been given the responsibility of carrying the rings, but not until they arrived at the unspecified venue, in case he lost them on the way.

Drew turned towards the sea, taking a deep breath. Caro would be coming for him. Carrying the small spark of life with her that would grow into their child. It was everything that he wanted, and he'd marry her anywhere that took her fancy.

Then he saw the boat. Bedecked with flowers, rounding the corner of the bay. And Caro. Standing at the prow, waving. Behind it was a small flotilla of boats, which were sounding their horns on the off chance that no one had noticed their presence. Drew started to run towards the dock, hearing Mav shouting with excitement behind him.

He couldn't take his eyes off her. Her blonde hair shimmering in the breeze. Her white dress moulding the curve of her hips and floating out behind her. The bouquet of summer flowers, bright in her hand, as she waved it above her head. It was Caro through and through, different and delightful, and he couldn't wait to be standing next to her.

Gramps steered the boat up to the dock and he jumped aboard before anyone had a chance to secure the mooring rope. Caro stepped carefully down from her perch, straight into his arms.

'Do you like it?' She looked up at him, her eyes dancing.

'I love it. I love *you*, Caro.' He found her hand, raising it to his lips.

'Shall we get married, then? We brought the registrar with us.' Caro gestured towards the local registrar, who was wearing a suit with a lifejacket and beaming at them from the deck.

'Yes. Let's get married.'

Phoenix, Lucas and Mav tumbled into the boat and they cast off, Gramps navigating the craft to the centre of the bay and then dropping the anchor. The other boats clustered around, forming a small floating cathedral bedecked with flowers under the wide arch of the summer sky. When it was time to say their vows, they faced each other, Caro clinging tightly to his hands as he steadied her against the roll of the sea. And when they were pronounced man and wife, a deafening chorus of horns sounded from the other boats.

Drew lifted his new wife out of the boat and onto the dock. The beach was beginning to fill up, with people who'd come overland from the village and family and friends from the boats. But all he could see was Caro. When she looked up at him, her eyes brimming with love, he knew for sure that he was the happiest man alive.

Their wedding day had been perfect. The food truck, which had raised a few eyebrows when it had arrived on the beach, had won everyone over with gourmet pancakes and delicious finger food, while another truck had dispensed drinks. The cake had been big enough to feed the whole village, and when darkness had begun to fall she and Drew had kicked off their shoes and danced together in the sand.

And now they were going home. They'd decided to spend the first few days of their marriage here, and then two nights in Florida, visiting Caro's parents for a second celebration. Then, ten days in the Caribbean, with nothing to do but relax and be together.

'What was your favourite thing?' Caro asked the question as Drew drove back towards the village.

'Hmm. Not sure. Mav almost dropping the rings overboard? Phoenix trying to snack on your bouquet?'

'What! All the things that went wrong, you mean.' Caro smiled. They'd been two of her favourite things too.

'What could possibly have gone wrong? You married me, didn't you?'

'I did. And you married me straight back.'

'Yes, I did.' Drew stopped the car outside their house, leaning over to kiss her. 'How could I do anything different when you came sailing across the sea to find me?'

He got out of the car, opening the tailgate to let Phoenix out and then folding her in his arms. 'Our home. Our family.'

'My lover...' Caro intimated his soft Cornish burr, and Drew laughed.

'Yes. Always.'

The house, up in the hills above Dolphin Cove, had come onto the market just a few months ago. It was perfect, big enough for the family that they both wanted, along with a book-lined study for Drew and even an old conservatory at the back, which could be renovated as a workshop for Caro. Drew had pulled out all the stops to make sure that the sale would go through in time for him to carry her over the threshold after their wedding. He lifted her up gently into his arms and Caro clung to him.

'You don't have to carry me all the way up the front path. That's just showing off, Drew.'

'I've been thinking about this for a long time now. I'm not doing it by halves.'

His leg was fully healed now, and Drew could do everything he'd done before the accident. He strode up the path, stopping at the front door.

'Keys. In my pocket.'

Caro felt in his pocket to find the door keys and unlocked the front door. Drew kicked it open and Phoenix bounded past him. Then he carried her over the threshold.

'*This* is my favourite part of the day.' She snuggled in his arms, kissing him.

'Yeah. Mine too.'

* * * * *

LET'S TALK

Romance

For exclusive extracts, competitions
and special offers, find us online:

f facebook.com/millsandboon

⊙ @millsandboonuk

🐦 @millsandboon

Or get in touch on 0844 844 1351*

For all the latest titles coming soon,
visit millsandboon.co.uk/nextmonth